blacke

a fiction novel by

reagan rothe

Black Rose Writing

www.blackrosewriting.com

ISBN: 978-0-9821012-7-8

Library of Congress Control Number: 2010904530

PUBLISHED BY BLACK ROSE WRITING

www.blackrosewriting.com

Printed in the United States of America

blacke is printed in 12-point Palatino Linotype

Praise for *blacke*

"Masterfully written, *blacke* is a welcome contribution to the mystery genre. An enthralling tale, a complex story line, and an emotional attachment to the characters make *blacke* a must read."
—*New Great Books*

"Rothe gives us a wonderfully descriptive ride through the character's mindset as he copes with each impending event."
—*Suspense Magazine*

"This happens to be the first novel of Rothe's that I have read. I can promise you it will not be the last. His eye for detail and sense of timing put the reader right in the scene, drawing in as if sharing an intimate encounter. I recommend this book wholeheartedly."
—*The Author's Lounge*

"It was dark and quirky and hinted at something so sinister that it would make your blood turn cold... and yet, I simply wanted more more more..."
—*The Novel Blog*

"Rothe's ability to show us the darkness within in contrast to the fresh, vibrant settings is astounding. Rothe has developed characters in *blacke* that will be remembered more for their flaws and short-comings than on their decisions and motivations."
—*PPS, Brian Knight*

This book is dedicated to my
beautiful wife, Minna Rothe.
She entered my life as an eternal light,
a beacon in my dark world.

My love for her will never be
expressed through words, but I will
continue trying for the rest of our lives.
I love you so much, Minna.

Special thanks to my mother,
Lindy, for instilling the art within me.
She paints... I write.

And to my English teacher,
Mrs. Moos, for revealing the gift
I now bestow upon you, the reader.

Foreword

by Jason Simmons

I have known Reagan Rothe for nearly a decade. He continues to amaze me with his creative writing abilities, a talent for understanding the human condition and his ability to systematically design true life stories, poems and fictional novels that twist the minds of readers; fulfilling our desire to be entertained.

Blacke is a unique tale of character tragedy, human emotion, flaws and the covert agendas of human beings. *Blacke* touches your heart by displaying the essence of love and death via suspenseful and haunting mystical epilogue; all of which makes it hard to put down any one of Reagan Rothe's thoughtfully written novels.

Reagan's aspiration and motivation to give readers an interesting twist on real life is unprecedented, as he does through interpretation of life experiences within his fictional writing. He continues to test the boundaries of traditional novel writing. He gives us a peak into the wicked mind of a character haunted by his past, attempting to overcome the most debilitating human experiences and enduring the worst human tragedies.

While being healed through coincidental love, hardcore dedication to basic human desires, passions and unwitting serendipitous relations, Mr. Blacke struggles to maintain basic structure in his life. *Blacke* is true to its own name. The dearth of happiness we all struggle with, at times, and triumphantly overcoming life's "darkness," is painted in *blacke's* fictional ink canvas.

In Mr. Blacke's world of irony and coincidental life struggles, he tries to overcome his own demons that haunt him from day break to dusk. Reagan Rothe's *blacke* will tantalize your need for validation as a human being, without the walls protecting the darkest side of your mind...

—Jason Simmons, MS, BCBA
Board Certified Behavior Analyst

<u>CEO and Founder:</u>
Clinical Behavior Analysis, LLC: Innovative Solutions to Modern Behavior Disorders

University of Texas at Austin (UTA) Research Associate (Ph.D. Doctoral Fellow)

"Making common sense more common."

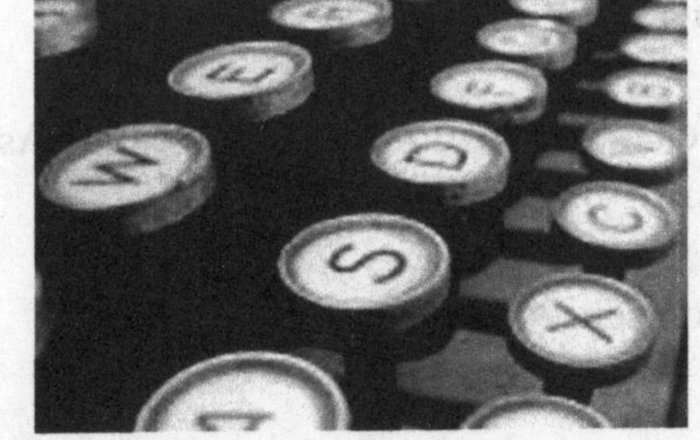

<u>chapter one</u>

The words move across the page like a bulleting train heading East, row by row... line after line... one sentence and then another. He's working on his new masterpiece, *All Roads Lead to Damascus*; already projected a bestseller by the likes of such prestigious newspapers as the *New York Times*, the *Washington Post*, and *USA Today*, to simply name a few.

The man turns... and there, standing behind him all smiles, the girl with the autumn-fire hair. Why would she be smiling? Why? After all that has happened to her in this demented world — this wretched town called Damascus.

No one really knows. This heart of man. The evil within, eating and stripping one's soul of their past premonitions without any cause, leaving a blackened void of ill-willed deceit. The fear rises in the pit of his stomach as the girl — all smiles — continues to arouse his persistent curiosity. He opens his mouth to speak. Nothing.

She turns away from him, and then calmly says these words, beneath her breath. "You never should have—"

The loud, thunderous clang of bronze meeting ancient oak disrupts his thoughts. The man stops typing on his antique typewriter, a family heirloom passed through generations. It is his favorite keepsake. The crisp keys whiter than any he'd seen before, capped with a perfectly thick layer of enhanced ivory. It is his favorite device for putting words to pages. Forget the computer. He cocks his head in the direction of the mansion's vast foyer, something he likes to call the 'Great Passageway' leading to the many doors of his realm.

What time is it? he thinks, lifting his fingers from the keys for the first time in hours. *I know I left the gates open for some reason... just can't remember why?* He stretches his hands wide as if he were ready to crush someone's skull. He then leans back in his 'Medieval Throne,' another pet name for something a little less dramatic. Although, his "writing" chair is rather overwhelming, with its back-lined, crushed red velvet and its jewel-encrusted wooden arms and legs. Throwing his arms into the air like a prophet beckoning to the gods, he rocks forward out of the "throne" and stands.

For the second time, the banging on the front door startles him. *I'm coming… I'm coming.* Leaving his octagon-shaped office, on the west wing of the mansion, the man heads through a door to the northern part of the house before turning to his right down a long, narrow hallway, lined with glass-cased shelves, dust free, carrying shadowbox-themed memoirs and his lifetime of writing accolades. These memoirs, unlike the east wing, carry only *his* past, and not his family's. This hallway, although notoriously long day or night, seemingly grows and haunts as the hour passes and the light from the west window shines no more.

But daylight has just begun, as scattered strands of the sun's beams portray a shadow on the wooden-planked floor before the traveling writer. It wasn't too long ago when this constricted hallway echoed with a child's laughter. But that's just a faded memory of what was… and what will never be again.

The knocking occurs a third time; the man shakes his head as he comes to another door at the end of the hall. *A little patience my persistent friend.* This door opens into the

'Great Passageway,' and the man turns to his right again and proceeds to the front of the luxurious mansion. He arrives at the main entrance, which towers above any six-foot person, with heavy oak double-doors and a half-circle finish at the peak; one might think there would be a portcullis and a moat waiting outside.

He raises the rustic iron latch, drawing free the lock, and then tugs on the circular brass handle (appearing like a bull's nostril ring) fastened to the door to his right, and the visitor's left. The door slowly cracks open, revealing new light in the mansion's foyer. Before the writer stands a nervous-looking fellow with a pen in one hand and a clipboard full of papers in the other. A reflecting piece of a silver recorder exposes itself at the top of his tan, sport's jacket's chest pocket. Sweat beads on his balding head, running down his forehead and into his beady eyes behind his perfectly-round rimmed glasses.

"Mr. Blacke?" the shaky visitor asks, dabbing his face with his striped tie. He scratches a small spot of hair along the side of his scalp, directly behind his right ear. He smiles, but it's not a confident one.

"That's me," Mr. Blacke answers, shrugging his shoulders and exposing the palms of his hands as to say 'I'm harmless.' Mr. Blacke raises one eyebrow and waits for the suited man to get on with it. The man squirms beneath his own fear of meeting someone idolized. But also… someone who has been deemed rather *different*.

"I don't mean to bother you, or… umm… take much of your time, sir, but if you could answer a few quick questions—" the man basically interrupts himself, taking a deep breath and starting over again, "—Excuse me, let me introduce myself. My name is Ray Spencer."

He extends his hand through the 'magical opening' separating the outside world from Mr. Blacke's domain and finishes by saying, "I'm new with the *Lago Diablo News*, and I know we haven't truly met here in town, but it's an absolute honor to meet such a distinguished… and great… writer."

You want to come inside, suck it a little more, buddy?

"I'm flattered, Mr. Spencer," Mr. Blacke chooses the second response, even though his initial thoughts were quite funny and tempting. He smiles more at his own humor inside his mind than from meeting this Ray Spencer fellow, but regardless of the realism behind it, the easing gesture seems to slightly calm the… *the reporter maybe?* "You wanted to ask a few questions, come inside."

Mr. Blacke steps aside of the doorway and motions for the fellow from the *Lago Diablo News* to enter. He closes the heavy door, shutting out the sun and leaving only trickles of the color-changing light spectrum to warp its way in, near the twenty-foot ceiling via small, decorative windows.

"This is more than I could have ever imagined," Spencer adds, nearly breaking his neck as he scans the cathedral ceiling and majestic artwork hanging from the high walls.

Alright, maybe I'll just put the tip in…

Mr. Blacke smiles behind his guest, always able to entertain himself when others can't quite get it done. He begins to pat the fellow on the back, but then thinks better of it. Don't want to conjure up any more visions than necessary. Don't want to extend a warm hand where a friendship would be lacking.

He takes the lead, heading to the end of the 'Great Passageway' and passing many doors to his left and right. Before reaching that end, they pass a twisting staircase—each individual step tiled with a sheet of solid marble—that travels straight up to a dark hole cut out of a recessed ceiling lower than the initial, domed covering. Once arriving at the back of the incredible foyer, another set of double doors await, smaller and less intimidating, but standing out in a contrasting and magnificent manner nonetheless. These doors are a glowing white, almost whiter than white. They stand alone at the finish to the intentionally dark foyer, bringing about some sort of soothing escape from when one might have thought there wasn't any. The entryway itself is dark, along with most of its satirical, ancient religious paintings, and then the colors in the room, also shadowy.

But there, leading into the grand dining room, is an ironic transition. Turning both silver handles and simultaneously pushing both doors open, Mr. Blacke says, "Waah-lah."

Speechless, Ray Spencer's eyes re-adjust to the bright light dazzling through at least a dozen, vertically long pane windows. Before the windows, a banquet-sized table engulfs the room, capable of seating more than twenty people. The craziest part about the dining table is that it appears to be one piece. 'How in the hell did someone get that thing in here?' the reporter thinks.

As though Mr. Blacke was reading his mind, "Got that table in Wales. Has some sort of ties with Robert the Bruce, but I'm not entirely sure which one or the actual story behind it. Anyways, when I built this house in ninety-six, I had the floor put in this room before the walls. And then the table was put in. And then they built the walls and windows—" Mr. Blacke circles and motions all around him, "—And everything else around the table. It cost me more than I made on my last novel to get it shipped here from Europe in one piece and then put it in this resting place."

"Amazing," the only word that comes to the reporter's mind.

"That… it is," Mr. Blacke responds, motioning for his guest to take a seat—the chairs were also composed entirely of wood, although they boasted sealed cedar, a more local find. Before the interview for the *Lago Diablo News*, the small-circuited newspaper covering the 2,286 that populate the town and several other smaller, surrounding towns including Redstone, Wickerton, Montaville, and Incarnate, begins, Mr. Blacke provides further background to the monumental dining table.

He tells the reporter that the wood used for the table is birch, which is, at least Mr. Blacke was told, the most common tree in Scotland. Somehow or another, the giant table was transported from Scotland by someone with ties to royal blood to Wales as a gift. For whom the gift was given by or received by, nobody exactly knew. But it was enough history to make the table itself worth millions. Two million to be exact. And then another seven-hundred grand shipping it across the Atlantic. But that was chump change for Mr. Blacke, who not only made millions with his ability to make words turn to life, but was also one of the largest shareholders and percent owners of a major oil and fuel company, called Simmons, Inc. Not to mention the *other* money—cash—resting beneath a trap door in the east wing's octagon playroom.

The actual interview began.

"Mr. Blacke, as I told you before," Spencer says, pressing record on the silver tape recorder now resting on the coated birch. With pen in hand, and a clipboard full of notes laying in front of him, also for jotting down new information, he continues, "The *Lago Diablo News* would love to get some of your thoughts and umm… inspiration behind the new novel. Or as you've referred to it in the *Times*… the new masterpiece. I'm hoping that since we *are* your local newspaper—"

Mr. Blacke stands, leaving the head of one end of the table, and walks to the other end. He picks up a newspaper—*Lago Diablo News*—and waves it back at Spencer, who hasn't said a word since Mr. Blacke got out of his chair. The reporter laughs, not entirely sure what's amusing, but as an instinctive reaction. Mr. Blacke comes back to the interviewing end of the table, careful not to bump his head on the side of a golden, dimly-lit chandelier, with sparkling crystals, dangling above and slightly hanging over each side of the centerpiece below it. The expensive décor reminds the author of a red deer's antlers, hanging upside down, but with full tines and captivating horned cups at the crest.

"Just wanted to let you know that I was a reader," Mr. Blacke says, referring to the newspaper as he returned to his seat.

"And we appreciate that, sir," Spencer replies, still not understanding the reasoning behind Blacke's peculiar ways.

Mr. Blacke rubs his chin with one elbow on the table. He waits for the reporter to commence with the questioning, but as soon as Ray Spencer opens his mouth to talk again, Mr. Blacke rises out of his chair, pushing it backwards, and asks, "Coffee?"

He makes an apologetic hand gesture as the reporter responds with a 'No, thank you.' He turns towards the west side of the mansion and walks a few steps to a swinging bar door, something that could have been the entryway into the O.K. Corral. The doors spray open with a gentle push, and Mr. Blacke turns back around, visible from the neck up and from the shins down.

"Sorry, one second, I need some coffee," he disappears behind the wall. Spencer sits in disbelief, not sure whether to take the interruption as something rude or something rather silly. He patiently waits, staring out the perfectly-rowed windows, flawless in both design and picturesque view. He scans the verdant valley, a mere seventy feet beyond the backyard, plush and abundant with rich trees and plants. The yard, groomed like a fresh haircut, smoothly rolls right down into the hollow below, but rises up on each side gently with tumbling, green mounds.

Further down the glen is a small pond. The sun glistens off the calm water and reflects all the way back up to the mansion's windows like a sparkling diamond in the rough. The scenery makes Spencer think that he has been misled into a magical grove hidden in a veiled rainforest—the variety of tropical plants and fruits dotted around the water's edge is quite lush. He's not sure that everything in it could possibly be real? Be that of unmatched beauty? Spencer is especially curious to how the southern-hemisphere plants survive the harsh winters. Little did he know that if the freeze comes on too hard, the following spring, Blacke simply has the trees dug up and replaced with new ones.

"This is kitchen number one," Mr. Blacke yells from out of sight, now disrupting Spencer from his own task at hand—admiring the view. "In case you were taking notes on the house."

"That's interesting," Spencer replies, speaking louder

than he's accustomed to. He guesses that the insight behind the 'number one' part would lead someone to speculate there's something more. So he asks, "There's two kitchens, then, I'm presuming?"

"Of course," Mr. Blacke responds.

"Of course," Spencer mutters to himself, mockingly. He continues to speak beneath his breath, "Doesn't everyone have two kitchens? It's perfectly normal, isn't it?"

He shakes his head at his own words, and then continues the conversation as he begins to think that Mr. Blacke isn't going to say anything else without first being provoked.

"Where is the second kitchen, Mr. Blacke?"

"It's through the swinging doors on the opposite side of the dining room," Mr. Blacke shouts from "kitchen number one," pouring his espresso into a tall, black mug with the name *blacke* printed on the side in white, all lowercase. Spencer stares past the other end of the birch table, seeing another set of bar doors, very similar in size and color, but with slightly different carvings along the trim and inner peaks.

"That's the evil kitchen," Mr. Blacke says, now in a lower voice as he reenters the dining room through the swinging doors. He follows the comment with a forced chuckle, making Spencer slightly uneasy. The reporter doesn't want to delve into "kitchen number two" anymore; he's perfectly fine with leaving it at *the evil kitchen.*

Mr. Blacke smiles wide enough to show his perfectly white and straight teeth and then takes his seat once again, seeming to have already forgotten the mentioning of another kitchen—especially an evil one. Spencer plays right along, wanting to rejoin the interview that he previously briefly began. He quickly restarts the conversation along his destined path, not wanting Mr. Blacke to make anymore random remarks or get him sidetracked.

"We were discussing the idea of possibly sharing some new thoughts or inspirations… or anything that might be unknown yet to your fans and readers about yourself or the upcoming *masterpiece,*" Spencer finishes by making imaginary quotations for "masterpiece" with both hands in the air.

Mr. Blacke raises his coffee mug, blows gently along the edge, and then takes a thoughtful sip. He uses his second hand to aid in the process of placing the mug back on the table's surface. He then raps on the table with his knuckles and says, "We were?"

Ray Spencer is in disbelief. This wealthy writer, called a genius by many, and a legend by many more, appears completely oblivious to what's going on. Spencer wonders if other reporters, for larger newspapers, had this much trouble conducting a proper interview. Spencer just doesn't get it. He doesn't know what to say; Mr. Blacke has now struck him dumbfounded.

But Spencer begins again, nonetheless, thinking they might sit in silence if he doesn't break it. "Yes, sir, I do believe we were," he says. "Can I begin with a few questions?"

He waits for Mr. Blacke's response before pressing the record button on the recorder he earlier stopped while his interviewee was out of the room. The famous writer takes another sip of his coffee, this time a little longer than the time before. It must be cooling. The smell of cinnamon steams from the mug's insides.

"I'll tell you what," he finally says. "You let me tell you a quick story, and then I'll answer whatever questions you want me to."

Believing that a simple 'no' wouldn't get the interview anywhere, and not wanting to deal with the results of an empty article, Spencer says 'sure.' Mr. Blacke leans back in his chair and folds his hands behind his head. He stares out the windows, focusing on barely visible red birds near the pond's edge. Sparkles of water splash from their tirelessly flapping wings and emulate broken pieces of glass. One bird, an iridescent red, dives at another bird, this one smaller and marked with a faded shade of cherry on it's feathers. The startled bird tumbles along the shore, wetting more than just its beak. They continue to play, several more red birds and an out-of-place sparrow join the mix.

What seems like several minutes is really just several seconds, but the mansion's eerie silence forces Spencer to grow restless in his chair. The reporter shifts, adjusts his glasses, and waits for the author to begin.

"There was this guy, see," Mr. Blacke says. "He was a friend of mine. We fished together. We played golf together. We played cards together, years before this whole Texas Hold 'Em phenomenon took place. We traveled together. We bought stock, real estate, you name it... together. He stayed a bachelor, I got married. I told him things I never told anyone else in the world. He *knew* the consequences. He *knew* what could happen. But I suppose love makes people do stupid things.

"He was a trusted friend. Not merely an acquaintance or friend of a friend, but someone I really loved as a brother. What he did was wrong. And what he did afterwards... was chicken shit. Now maybe I had something to do with it, from a friendship level, not anything physically, of course. But let me ask you, have you ever had anyone close to you kill themselves?"

"No… I haven't. It must be devasta—" Spencer answers, but is interrupted before he can share any sympathies.

"It should be. Devastating. That is what you were going to say, wasn't it?" Mr. Blacke asks, but doesn't wait for a response. "But this time… it wasn't. The twisted bastard deserved death, and he simply chose to take the easy way out before someone else did it for him. Put that in your story. No, instead, forget about him. Go ahead, ask away."

The *Lago Diablo News* reporter, Ray Spencer, is now more puzzled than ever. Mr. Blacke says he wants to tell him a story, but where's the plot? Where's the moral? Where's the story altogether? The writer shared some thoughts—random and disjointed. But to say the least, Spencer is relieved. He is eager to truly begin the initial interview, wanting to get some unknown or new information that will dazzle his dedicated readers. But, excited as he may be, he simply can't help his trained probing.

"What was his name? Your friend?" Spencer inquires, hoping to find a deeper story farther down the line.

"Henry," Mr. Blacke says, and then smiles again, raising his brows. "Oh, Henry Lucas."

"Would you like to share more on Mr. Lucas?"

"There's nothing more to speak of there." Mr. Blacke's mind flashes with a passing image of his old friend. There he is, Henry Lucas, with his wavy brown hair, slept to the back or to the side to keep it out of his eyes, always appearing the eighty's country club member. He dresses the part as well, tailored suitpants and silk shirts. The image leaves Mr. Blacke like an autumn leaf being swept by a chilled breeze.

"Okay, fair enough." Spencer jots down the name *Henry Lucas* at the bottom of his clipboard notes. He had pressed stop on his recorder again, expecting the story to be something of little use. So for the third time, he presses record and hopes for a better result. "*All Roads Lead to Damascus,* you've mentioned in some of your other interviews about the ties between it and some of your previous great novels such as *When an Anagram Isn't a Margana, The Surrounding Sounds,* and *A Dozen Blacke Tales,* to just name a few, but *is* there truly more behind the symbolism and correlations?"

"There's always more behind the curtain," Mr. Blacke immediately answers, and then pauses for a brief time to collect his thoughts. The sides of Spencer's lips turn ever-so-slightly upward as he is pleased to have finally gotten the interview somewhat underway. "With that said… reading is like dreaming. You can misinterpret the words, or read them entirely wrong, and you envision something that is completely out of place with the writer's own view. If the writer doesn't paint the picture well enough, then the reader will have to use their own brush, stroking the canvas with amateur marks, but filling the emptiness regardless. That is the same with each writer's own symbolism. They may use similar names, references, places, simply because it comforts them, and they enjoy the ease in which those thoughts came back to them. Or they may use different names, wanting the reader to forget what they've done before and focus on something new. Something they believe isn't on the same timeline and not related at all. But that isn't entirely true. The correlations are there… parts of the world may change, but the whole world will remain."

Spencer, despite enjoying the writer's rambling philosophical bullshit, cannot believe how far Mr. Blacke's thoughts have diverted from the initial question. There's no answer in there. He's simply playing the part of a polished politician.

But not wanting to upset Mr. Blacke or push him too much, Spencer proceeds to the next question. "I see… uhh… you have some brilliant thoughts there, a great mind, Mr. Blacke. Is there anything that inspires you to write besides what you've given *us* fans and reporters before? Anything the people might not know?"

"Of course there is. For instance, sitting alone in my upstairs chamber with no light. The darkness prevailing from every corner. The only noise coming from a nineteen forty-seven record player with the initials *S.B.* engraved in the side. That engraving, obviously occurring many years later to the trained eye. The music… clearly opera. With that alone, the ideas and thoughts flood the brain like a raging river of light bulbs. Each one translucent, but then lighting up like a firefly with each inspirational wave, stopping by the cortex to say hello."

'More incredible bullshit,' Spencer thinks. He nods his head with a false approval. He had always read up on Mr. Blacke's previous interviews and articles, surprisingly enjoying the epic dialogue and witty use of tongue. But now that he was actually asking the questions, it wasn't so amusing. The worst part of it is that Spencer didn't know whether Mr. Blacke was dodging the questions entirely, hiding some dark secrets of the past or not wanting to expose any emotional truths, or that if Mr. Blacke really thought his answers were sincere and exactly what the audience wanted. I mean, hell. This is what Ray Spencer took pleasure from reading about. He found it encouraging at first, thinking that Mr. Blacke couldn't be merely a mortal man. His words were so remarkably spun that it took a lifetime to weave them. But now, in person. It just isn't the same. Something is wrong. Something is missing, hidden beneath this man's surface. 'The Evil Kitchen,' Spencer thinks. There's something more here.

"Is there more?" Mr. Blacke asks the asker. Spencer isn't sure if he's jokingly moving the interview along or if he truly believes he's done his service for now.

"Yes, surely," Spencer says.

b l a c k e

The headline in next week's issue of the *Lago Diablo News* reads as follows:

Blacke's Back, Writer Speaks on New Novel

The sound of classical opera fills Mr. Blacke's bedtime chamber as he shuffles poker chips on the chess table by the upstairs left bay window. He drops the chips and then quickly re-stacks them, creating a faint noise well below the blaring music, as he rocks in his rocking chair. Tapping his right foot on the hard floor, he keeps a steady beat with the music, near-perfect synchronicity. Beside him sits a double-king-sized bed with four individually carved spires (ancient Roman designs from the helms to shields to short swords, all detailed in the spiraling wood) supporting the decorative canopy and railing for a draw curtain to slide along.

He rocks without saying a word. This is *his* time for inspiration. *His* time for new thoughts. He is over eighty-percent finished with his masterpiece, *All Roads Lead to Damascus*, quite possibly his final work of art, but something is missing. The ending isn't exactly right. It must end with something special. A novel… a great novel… must not end with a whimper when the pages will total somewhere over fifteen-hundred. The reader will get their money's worth, you can bet on that. But for now, he must sit and contemplate this dilemma. It will come to him. It has before… always. And it will come again, this time better than ever, assuring his masterpiece of not only being the #1 bestseller, but also being one of the greatest books ever written. It will be resting aside some of his favorite novelists in the *Shelved Halls of the Afterlife*—Tolstoy, Hemingway, Twain, Puzo, King, to list a handful.

Why? Because it is his destiny. This is the path that has been trodden for him, lighted before him amidst a million cream-colored candles and then forced upon him like an apprenticeship. Whether it's a gift… or a curse… it's his to deal with. And it will come to him—nonetheless.

The sound of thunder is the first noise to disrupt his peaceful, personal form of meditation. The deep boom is followed by a streak of white light, jagging like countless z's outside his window. Soon after, heavy drops of rain begin there rap-a-tap beating against the thick glass and also against the extremely durable tile slate roof.

Mr. Blacke stops his rocking and smiles. He rises from the chair and heads towards the center of the mansion, opening the bedroom door along the way and descending the marbled, spiral staircase, allowing his hands to glide down the cold, circle-iron banister. He takes the rain outside, suspending his deep thoughts for later, as a sign.

I mustn't worry about the ending anymore tonight. Tomorrow brings a new day… with new hope. I might even make a trip to town…

All but the last part sounds convincing in his head. Especially since he's been thinking about taking a trip to town for over two years now. Ever since, well… we'll discuss *that* later. There is plenty of time for *that*.

The funny part is that despite it being such a long time ago, Mr. Blacke can vividly remember his last trip into Lago

Diablo. It might have had something to do with all the emotional events that followed that same day, but either way, his memory stood strong.

He had to run a few errands, mostly needing to mail some letters for his wife, Sierra. And also, pick up a few mismatched groceries. The couple weren't on the best speaking terms, but Mr. Blacke's wife was pretty good at relaying messages via a small, handwritten note or grocery list.

The first stage of the trip didn't take part in Lago Diablo; it, as a matter-of-fact, took place in Incarnate. The neighboring town due East, surrounded by tall pine trees and sharp hills.

Mr. Blacke had to run to a printing shop to pick up another package of special typing paper—no smear, no smudge, and strong enough to handle the violent banging of Mr. Blacke's typewriter keys. *I even remember what I was listening to...*

b l a c k e

The music blasted out the open windows of my beamer. My hair, thick and dark, rippled as the outside wind passed. My face felt of sandpaper, showing off a full five o'clock shadow. I tapped my fingers against the steering wheel to the beat of "Don't Fear the Reaper" by Blue Oyster Cult.

"C'mon baby…. and she had no fear…. and she ran to him," I sang, my bright yellow eyes hiding behind a new pair of Ray-Ban's. I was wearing a charcoal gray, "Goodfella's" gangster suit with a pair of nine-hundred dollar, black dress shoes shiny enough to blind someone. Or quite possibly, bright enough to return vision to someone lacking. I accelerated on the gas, the needle kissing ninety miles per hour.

The sign on Route 163 read—Incarnate 7, Montaville 22. I flew by, watching it immediately disappear from my rearview mirror. First stop… printing paper. And then grab a quick bite to eat at Sally's Café. The pecan pie was phenomenal, especially "a la mode." After that, it was back to Lago Diablo to pick up some groceries (milk, cream cheese, a couple of filet's, and a bottle of Silver Oak—one of my friends described the red wine as smooth, chocolate silk sliding down your throat) and filled prescriptions for Sierra. She didn't really need all the drugs that easily accessible, but who was I to stop her? Who was I to tell her how to deal?

And then finally, before heading back up the hill to the mansion, a quick stop at the Starr County Post Office to mail some of my wife's letters. It was easy enough. At least, the day on the town was. That night… something different. But that was another story for another time.

My new release, "When an Anagram Isn't a Margana," had just hit the shelves three weeks before and remained number one on the bestseller's list. It had already sold more than double the copies of the second-ranked novel, which had been out a week more. I had received high acclaims and praises from every key newspaper, reviewer, and editor around the world, including Kirkus and Library Journal and many more. Everyone knew this novel was going to be huge. Nobody, though, had guessed its success would set an all-time sales record for the first month.

I pulled into the all-trades store, hidden from the main road and without a sign featuring any business name. The owner was a fellow named Pete Vincenzo, an out-of-place Italian who started nearly every conversation with, 'you been watching the Sopranos lately?' before making some wisecrack and then trying to save face by saying, 'you know I'm just breakin' balls, right?' Pete carried a lot of specifically requested items, such as the high-grade typewriter paper. He special-ordered it strictly for me, and I always compensated him with a little extra green that drew the same remark every time, 'you need to add more pages to this masterpiece.'

To this day, I don't have any name for Pete's store. I had the phone number on an old business card, but the card only said "Pete Vincenzo" and gave a number and address. No store name.

It might possibly be something as simple as "Vincenzo's." But who knows? I haven't been there in over two years anyways. I phoned the store one time; from then on, Pete had someone deliver my paper. Not only did the runner get a nice tip, but I always threw in a little extra cash for Pete, not hearing that same remark out of his mouth anymore, but hearing it in my head, nonetheless.

I paid for my paper, tipping Pete, and then laughed as he said, "You need to add more pages, Mr. Blacke. If this is such a masterpiece, you need to keep on writing. Want me to order more paper?"

"Sure," I had said before leaving. I let the screen door close gently behind me, trying not to slam it. I could faintly hear Pete call one of his workers, possibly his son, a "fanuke," and laughed as I opened the door to my BMW. I had changed my mind about sitting down and eating. I really wasn't that hungry. But I stopped by Sally's Café anyways, since it was less than two miles up the road.

I ordered a slice of pecan pie for later, forced to leave off the homemade vanilla-bean ice cream because it would have melted in the Styrofoam box. Next stop... the Lago Food Mart.

The mixed CD in my car was now playing "Smoking in the Boy's Room," by Brownsville Station, not the Motley Crue cover, another classic from my younger days. I sped back West, staying to the far right when I reached the fork in the road. If you stayed on

163, you would circle around Lago Diablo and head to Wickerton. If you went left, you would head due south up the hill, and then a couple of miles, to my house at the peak.

But the road exiting to the right veered slightly northwest, and split the downtown section of Lago Diablo. There weren't many cars on the road, I only remember passing one—an old, rusty ranch truck appearing to be tugged along by an invisible rope. It couldn't have been going over thirty-five on the main road.

I left it in the dust, the pickup leaving my mirror almost as fast as the mile markers. I watched as the Starr County Post Office went by on my left, thinking, 'I'll stop by there on my way back through.' Windows down, wind whistling outside, I sang some more, "Teacher don't you fill me.... up with your rules.... everybody knows that.... smokin' ain't allowed in school."

The legal speed limit dropped rapidly as Lago Diablo's main strip drew into sight. There were two restaurants downtown, Barnaby's Barnacles, a seafood and steak joint with good oysters (fried or raw), and then the Lago Diner, owned by Doug & Betty St. Clair, the same couple who owned the Lago Food Mart. The St. Clair's were Lago Diablo. Their family spread wide; it probably caused some slight incest because the majority of all the teenagers were related one way or another. Your great-grandfather was my great-grandfather, your mom married my uncle, your sister married my first-cousin—some being blood, others just being *connected at the hip.*

Also downtown, there was Dan's Home Hardware, the Lago Diablo State Bank, and a community center-slash-dance hall. It was called the G.G. Center, after the man who built it many years back. It had been restored and upgraded several times along the way, and I couldn't recollect the fellow's name. Besides the ISD, home to the Lago Diablo Dragons, and some other scattered, specialized businesses, that pretty-much summed up the town. Hell, the biggest store in the area was north of here in Redstone. They had just finished building a Super Wal-Mart; the local residents didn't know things were so easy to get a hold of.

I parked the shimmering silver car in the side parking lot of the Lago Food Mart. Out of habit from living in urban areas, I readied my thumb to press the automatic lock button on my key ring, but then remembered where I was now. I had moved away from the big cities and big lights. I left the crowds of people where everybody wanted to know everything for the intimate town-life where everybody already thought they knew everything. Although rumors and false happenings were sometimes spread, for the most part, people could keep to themselves and mind their own business. Just a simple, friendly 'hello' followed by a 'how things doin'?' with a witty, but roundabout answer usually did the trick every time here in Lago Diablo.

"How things been doin', Mr. Blacke?" a young, blond-

haired man asked. I couldn't remember his name.

"Some days better than others, some fish bigger than others." It wasn't my best, but it would suffice. It was something my dad would tell me after our summer fishing trips to Lake Silstead. I never grasped any hidden meaning, but used it to this day, nonetheless.

The chap with peach fuzz laughed, not because he actually deliberated my response, but because I was a celebrity. The straight, honest truth. I chuckled back and gave a quick wave. I turned the old, brass knob on the door leading into the grocery store and heard the bell—connected above the threshold—dingle, announcing my presence.

The store wasn't crowded—a few regulars here and there either sitting along the tables in the back drinking coffee or tea or other customers running a few errands, as was I. I bumped into Tommy Shaw, a short and husky man with curly, uncombed hair. He had the top few buttons of his faded blue ranch shirt unbuttoned, allowing a patch of clumped hair that looked like the rough at Sawgrass to spill into sight.

Tommy was a talkative fellow, as with most jolly fat men. I could already see in his eyes that I wasn't going to get by him with just a simple, polite 'hello, how are you?' He started rambling on about this and that, and without missing a single beat, he wound up telling me one of his classic jokes. If I had been listening *intently, I would have caught on that the first part of his conversation was only a prologue to the actual joke itself—building hype where hype probably wasn't needed.*

The joke, if I remember correctly, featured a one-arm fisherman (it was ironic that I was just thinking about fishing trips with dad) winning some sort of big bass tournament. The punch-line... or kicker for others... was when Tommy said, 'the one-arm fisherman caught a fish THIS BIG!' and he held out only one arm to show the fish's size.

It really was a funny joke. I just hadn't felt like taking the time to fully attend to it. I laughed anyways. Tommy let out a roar that caused a few heads to peak around the corner to see what was going on in the aisle in which we were currently standing.

When I finally broke away from the conversation without being too unfriendly, I picked up the things Sierra had marked down on a printed, well-organized list. The milk, the cream cheese, the steaks, don't forget the bottle of Silver Oak (the last one in stock—I made sure to ask Mrs. St. Clair to order another case).

There wasn't any excitement during the last stop (post office) or the windy drive back up the hill to my mansion. "The Mansion on the Hill..." one magazine article deemed it. I couldn't quite remember which one, but I thought the name might make a good book title someday. If, that is, I could conjure up a story to back it up.

The Mansion on the Hill...

b l a c k e

There truly isn't any one reason Mr. Blacke hadn't traveled to town since that day. Of course, his wife, Sierra, died soon after. That is definitely some sort of cause behind it. And then, the gift—or curse—might play a part in the hermit's game as well. But who really knows?

"Who really knows?" Mr. Blacke asks, eager to hear the sound of something besides the rain still pattering against his window. He has been laying in bed awake for several hours. He reaches both arms out to their fullest length, stretching, but is still unable to find the outer edges of his massive mattress. The antique typewriter downstairs waits silently... alone, in darkness.

It waits for him. It waits for his fingers to move like a praying mantis' ritual dance of love. It calls... it beckons.

He thinks on the motives behind not ever leaving his castle. There are many, true. But trying to put one's finger on something solid, to pinpoint the exact explanation, is something Mr. Blacke has been trying to do with his "award-winning" novels throughout the years. But with one's own life, things aren't always as easy as changing a sentence here and rearranging a chapter there or retyping a new ending to either enhance the entire story or give the reader some sort of hope, where in their own life, hope may be bleak.

So instead of sleeping, he welcomes the threatening insomnia with arms open and a winner's grin on his face. The smile that says, 'I've got secrets. I know things that are hidden behind the mask. I know more than I've ever let on or revealed.'

Mr. Blacke folds his hands behind his head—resting on two down pillows—and stares up at himself. The smudge and streak-free mirror beckons at him from above, hanging atop his bed's wraparound frame below the vaulted ceiling. He sees himself smiling because of his unimaginable success. He sees himself smiling because it's easier to hide the demons that stir at night than to try and fight them. He sees himself smiling because of his life's accomplishments—any single one of his many would make an average person fulfilled. He sees himself smiling because…

He's Mr. Blacke…

And you're not—

M

chapter two

I was a young boy in 1978, living in a small town called Augur, just old enough to realize a girl could be something beautiful, but still innocent enough to not care. Girls were girls, boys were boys, they didn't coexist, yet. Plus, they had cooties and all kinds of germs.

There were the sweet summer days of baseball, America's pastime, with sweat glistening off youthful cheeks and rolling down their red, sandy faces. Scabbed knees and elbows, waiting to showcase a hidden cherry beneath the glorifying uniform. Smells of cotton candy and popcorn, quenched by a tall Coca-Cola on ice. Signs from the third-base coach, touching his shoulder, touching his nose, pressing a finger against his chin, and then banging closed fists together, signaling bunt or hit-and-run.

I remember tipping my Cherokees' ballcap at some passing girls as a couple of friends of mine and I were headed out for some fun after chalking up a nice, 8-4 victory over the feared Red Riders. I played shortstop and had a two-run homer in the game. But the team's success was more important to me. If I had to compare myself to a modern-day big leaguer, I would have said my style was like that of Derek Jeter's. Except, of course, Jeter went on to play for the Yankees on the biggest stage of them all, a future hall-of-famer for sure on my ballot. I went on to write...

Freddy Fingers, our second baseman, nicknamed because of his abnormally large digits, belched at the four pony-tailed blondes and brunettes. I laughed, right along with our starting pitcher, Jake Snake. *His nickname? More than just a silly rhyme?* At least, not to my knowledge.

We left the ballpark and street lights behind, strolling out of town. We passed the grove of sycamore trees, and the three of us hung out down by Otter Creek. We skipped stones in the brackish water, seeing who could get the most splashes. Jake, using his great pitching arm, stayed true to form, winning the dubious contest with an impressive eleven rock bounces.

We made jokes and laughed. Most of them were references to each other's moms, grotesque without any limitations. 'Your mom is so fat...' or, 'Your mom is so ugly...' or, 'Your mom is so poor...' and on and on.

We ditched the uniforms, stripping down to our tights or under shorts for a quick swim before the sun set. I remember the old, multi-knotted swinging rope hanging from a thick branch, high up a towering pine. We took turns doing our best kamikaze-like jumps, or better yet, reckless crashes into the deepest part of the blue-green water. Whichever kids weren't currently jumping would rate the jumper on a scale from one-to-ten. The highest score I ever remember receiving was a solid nine for my signature "reverse spinner" off the rope.

Just before dark, we headed home. Jake and I said goodbye to Freddy first, as he lived in a wooden cottage on the outside of town. Our two houses were separated by only a couple of blocks, located in a downtown area called Shady Oaks. This was the middle-class neighborhood in Augur, my hometown. The super-rich kids lived up on the hill, adjacent to the school district. Their mansions and multi-story homes, some resembling Civil War plantations with mossy oaks and weeping willows, were tree-lined and high-fenced with menacing double gates. Their lawns were always perfectly cut; the smell of mowed grass tickled our noses as we walked to class.

One house, a three-story country-style, was my favorite, mostly because of its jet black horses roaming the meadows and stopping to drink at a trickle of refreshing water zig-zagging through the property. A beautiful wrought-iron bridge, the color of sable, with sealed teakwood planks, transcended the skinny waterway, just wide enough for exotic cars to pass over.

But back in Shady Oaks, in the middle-class world, Jake said farewell as he pushed open his wooden-picket gate and sprinted down the sidewalk to his humble homestead. I waved goodbye and jogged down the road, scattered with falling leaves. The few streetlights in my neighborhood had already turned on, providing plenty of light for my nightly trot home. My house really wasn't all that bad. Compared to the mansions on the hill, it seemed quite small. But in contrast to the black kids' shacks and broken down brick homes, it was more than a child could ask for. Jesse Wymes, our starting centerfielder, had taken a few of us baseball players to his house one day after a game. We couldn't believe how many siblings and cousins and however-related people could bed up in one place. It seemed miserable. But, as humans tend to do when they know nothing else, they adjust and make the best of things.

My house *did* have a wraparound porch. My dad loved to relax in his over-sized rocking chair, smoking a long pipe and watching the nearby Howser kid spray his younger brother with the garden hose every time he got the chance. This gave my dad a good chuckle. No harm, no foul. If there was someone seriously being injured or bullied, my dad would have stepped in immediately and dealt out a solid lashing. But boys will be boys.

I was an only child. Later on in life, I would continue the tradition by having only one son with my wife, Sierra. But right now, it was just me and Smokey, my chocolate-brown, pure Golden Retriever. He had a thick coat of hair that shined only after a fresh wash; it was mostly snagged with an assortment of different stickers and smelled of whatever he could find to roll in. But he was mine... and I loved him.

He camped out in the backyard, sleeping in a doghouse composed of barn wood and a mismatched tin roof. Since the time my parents had first gotten me Smokey, my dog and I had played at least once a day. Who needed girls when one could always rely on 'Man's Best Friend.'

I truly loved the breaded beast, more costly than the rest of the neighborhood mutts. I loved his doggy smell and slobber from his big black gums that splashed on my cheeks as he licked my face. He pawed me with such trust... such admiration. We had a special bond.

That's what made me realize, for the first time in my life, I was empty inside.

It wasn't that I didn't feel things. It wasn't that I didn't share remorse, or pity, or grief. I felt all those things and more. I just had something missing inside me. A black hole, if you may. Something that allowed me to set my feelings aside like a boring read. Sometimes I would come back to them, giving them another chance. But in the end, my needs always came foremost.

Was it really my needs? Perhaps, it was my destiny? I didn't know what was still to come... yet.

I didn't feel that I was a bad person. Or a bad kid for that matter. I just wasn't a good person. It could be summed up as simple as that. After all, I never truly knew if anything that happened around me was entirely my fault or one coincidence after another.

I arrived at the front gate, lifting the rusty latch out of its locking device and allowing the hinged contraption to sway open. I saw my dad, rocking as usual.

"Hey Morty," he called from his chair on the stain-sealed porch. It was short for Morton. "You're late for dinner."

"I know," I said, taking my ballcap off and ascending the three steps to the front door. "We won our game, though!"

"That's great, Morty. Any hits?"

"Yeah! You betcha'! I had a two-run blast and a

double."

"Fantastic," my father said, rising from his lulling motion. "Be careful in there, though—" my dad pointed in the direction of inside the kitchen part of the house "—mom's not as forgiving as I when it comes to being late for her hard-prepared supper. If we had it her way, we would have started without you. But I said I needed a smoke, trying to buy you some extra time."

We exchanged smiles. I could always count on my pops. I always wanted to tell him my future secrets, above all others, but never could come to it. He died of heart failure before I ever had the courage. On one hand, I didn't know if he'd even believe me. On the other hand, I couldn't bare to see the disappointment if he did.

"Thanks, dad," I said, holding the screen door open for him as he walked inside first. He messed up my already unfixed hair with his left hand as he passed. I waited for a comment like, 'you need to cut those black locks, they're getting too long,' but didn't get one this time.

I took mom's wrath full stride, swallowing my tongue and letting her bark tiresome remarks. She didn't understand baseball. She didn't understand boys being boys and playing after playing. She had grown up with all girls, her own father dying when she was only seven. Somewhere, further down my life's path, I was told that girls had it different from boys; even when they got older, they were expected to do the right thing.

Plus, telling my mother about my future successes and the demons that lured in the shadows, always revolving around the writing, seemed completely out of the question. Where I contemplated sharing my thoughts with my father, me sharing with my mother never entered my mind.

After eating meatloaf and potatoes, chugging a glass of milk with the meal, I headed out back to play with Smokey before homework and bedtime.

A good dog carries a trait that humans take for granted—the ability to smile and be happy regardless of what's going on around them. They rush to your side, anxious to greet you each and every time and welcome your rubbing hands and pleasant words. A person could learn a lot about the simplicity of life from a canine. Sleep, eat, shit, and enjoy. Forget about the damn bills.

Smokey and I played for half an hour. Once back inside, before heading to my room, a news clip caught my attention from the television. My mom and dad were sitting on the light-blue sofa, sporting a couple of spaghetti stains from some of my messier days of eating, and a large, dark coffee stain from my dad. I heard the name of my favorite baseball player being mentioned—Dwight Evans.

Topps, a baseball-card trading company, had supposedly placed a special, *one-card printed only*, card of the Red Sox outfielder in one of its newer, flashier packs. The 1973 rookie card, of my favorite player if I hadn't already mentioned it, was projected to be one of the highest valued cards in recent times.

Not only was Dwight Evans a good, rising player, but when there's only one, distinct card, featuring any athlete, it's going to heighten the price. In this case, the experts were expecting big things for the lucky kid who bought the special pack.

That special kid...

Was me, Morton Blacke.

b l a c k e

I went to bed that night, wishing for that card.

I could see it come to life, right before my eyes. Dwight Evans swings the lumber and doubles into the power alley. He races to first, taking a wide turn around the bag. His helmet tumbles off his head as he prepares to slide into second with a two-bagger. The sport of baseball—a thing of beauty.

Before steroids. Before the government interfered. Money in their pockets. What business was it of theirs? There were bigger issues in the world—in the U.S.—than performance-enhancing drugs. But that's a story for another book.

I don't remember if I felt anything special that night—wishing upon every star in the sky for that one, Dwight Evans' rookie card. This collectible wouldn't be going into my bicycle spokes as a comical noisemaker, you could bet on that. That was for the washed-up Joes and one-season has beens. They lined my Schwinn's tires, better than any pack of Hoyle's.

I don't want to get sidetracked. That was the easy part... throughout my entire life. I could always find a way to change the subject with my brilliant dialogue; half the time, the person speaking to me never even knew it happened. They called me a genius. They called me a master of writing. They called me peculiar. They called me many names, but never got it quite right.

I didn't know if I truly was or wasn't? That is for you to decide. But they *never* called me a monster.

Like I said, I didn't feel different. I got up in the morning—the Red Sox outfielder on my mind. I washed my face. I brushed my teeth. I combed my hair, which was darting in every which way, looking like it needed an escape. I went to eat breakfast with my mother.

My dad had already vacated the premises. He left before 6 a.m. to supervise down at the coal mine. He was the first-ranked officer down at Shaft 7. I missed him in the mornings. Believe me, I loved my mother dearly, but for the most part, we didn't have much to say to each other. It always seemed like forced words. One of us thinking something off-topic and then saying it with a false enthusiasm.

The worst part... the absolute worst part was when she tried to actually pretend she loved baseball. She acted like she knew the game, and would question me about a specific team and player, usually only repeating something she had heard a sport's reporter say earlier that morning. I was just a young lad, but I thought it was so pathetic. She should stick to her mom things. They weren't my favorite topics, but at least they were real.

I distinctly remember this one time, when mom said something like, 'can you believe *that* Billy Martin pulled Reggie out of the game like that, showing him up in front of the fans? Wasn't that Bush League?'

I said something like, 'you don't even know what Bush

League is?'

And she only ended the conversation, saying, 'well... it was.'

I didn't push the envelope. Frankly, she had no idea what she was even talking about. And I was a Red Sox fan anyways, what did I care about the Yankees? The Evil Empire?

Everything was as normal on this day as any other day. I kissed my mom goodbye after drinking two glasses of milk, for my bones, and downing three pieces of cornbread with butter and honey. It wasn't the store-bought honey either, this sticky substance came from the local bee man, a friend of my father's.

I rode my bicycle to school that day, sporting a Boston Red Sox ballcap and listening to the consistent hum of my crappy baseball cards twang the spokes. On some occasions, I would walk with fellow teammates and friends. And then other times, I rode my bike. It just depended on the mood. Or how late I was.

Nothing out of the ordinary happened at school or during the Augur Cherokees' baseball practice. I told several of my baseball friends about the special on the *Topps'* card, featuring Dwight Evans. We had a group of about five prepared to head down to Gold's Trading Store after practice. And five it was.

I was prepared to buy all the baseball card packs I could afford. If my math is still correct, let's see... fifteen cents a pack, I had a little over two bucks in change, that comes out to around fourteen packs or so. It didn't really matter. I only needed one.

This was how the entire racket went down.

I remember hearing *Hotel California* playing in the store when I said, "This is the magic pack, boys and girls, right here." I picked the third pack down in the *Topps'* card box. It was neatly placed with the other trading cards on the bottom shelf of the section of Gold's Trading Store that had all the sporting cards and some fantasy cards, as well as the smokes and tobacco.

"You're so full of shit, Morty," Kip Lawson said, a friend of mine and the Cherokees' rightfielder. He grabbed his crotch with his right hand and added, "I've got your magic pack right here."

All five of us cracked up until Jake Snake pretended to hit Kip in the nose. The rightfielder flinched, and then Jake gave him two in the shoulder. "Two for flinching, fag."

"Yeah, yeah, you got me," Kip replied, rubbing his left shoulder from the slight pain.

"Hey! Check this out!" That was Joey Smalls, trying to

get our attention. Joey had a history of taking Kip's jokes and one-upping them. And this was no exception. The boy had snuck over to one of the checkout counters and stolen a large salted pickle from the unattended jar by the register. He then came by to our group and prepared himself by unzipping his dirty jeans and sticking the pickle half-in and half-out. That's when he called out.

Seeing the pickle-penis, I laughed my buns off, right with the others. But the laughter had only started. We were fairly loud, but not loud enough to cause any unwanted attention. But when Freddy Fingers snatched the pickle-penis from out of Joey's fly and took a bite, that's when the fracas came full circle. Our laugher echoed through the store, bringing on that stinging sensation that tickled your belly. Jake Snake hit the deck, rolled around, and slapped the floor.

That's when Mr. Weeks, the storeowner, came over. He was balding, sported a beergut, and didn't really like kids, especially those that caused trouble in his store. Freddy, Joey, Kip, and I silenced, waiting for Mr. Weeks to make the next move. Jake held his hands over his mouth, twisting on the ground and trying to contain his own hysterics when Mr. Weeks kicked him in the ribs.

He hopped to his feet like a boxer trying to beat the ten-count. He smiled and said, "Yessir." Even though nothing had been said.

"G'damn wight, sum-bitch," Mr. Weeks swore like a sailor. And his slight lisp made it hard to keep from laughing again. He then pointed at Freddy and said, "Yew gonna' pay fer dat pickle, son."

Joey Smalls added, "He sure is, sir. That's what I told 'em."

I smiled, thinking again that Joey was the one who took the pickle in the first place. We all stared at Mr. Weeks, but no one moved.

"Now yew' boyz keepit don, or I'll's run you outta' ere."

"Yes, sir," we said in harmony. Mr. Weeks went behind the main counter, leaving us.

Freddy pushed Joey's head and said, "Asshole."

I couldn't wait any longer. Before the gang could even gather around, I ripped open the pack.

And on the very top, it beckoned...

"Holy shit!" Kip Lawson shouted.

"No fuckin' way!" Jake Snake added, his bulging eyes bigger than giant gum balls.

"Unbelievable!" Joey Smalls exclaimed, raising his arms high in the air.

"This is the craziest shit I've ever seen!" Freddy Fingers

joined in the excitement, slapping me on the back and almost knocking the Dwight Evans' card from my grasp.

It rested, face up, in the palms of both of my hands. I coveted the special card. With four dear friends circling me, already on the look out for any suspicious behavior around us, Dwight Evans wasn't leaving my sight. The card was mine.

I had wished for it, feeling deep inside of me that this was something I had to have. I had never wanted something that badly before; I had never yearned for any object with such a greedy, selfish demeanor. Or was it?

I didn't do anything wrong. I didn't hurt anyone, did I? I only wished for something, and as good luck would have it, I got it. I was a fortunate kid, right? It's okay for others to be jealous or envy my Dwight Evans', outfielder for the Boston Red Sox, card, but they can't blame me for wanting something. I was a child. I wanted lots of things. It just so happened... I wanted this card more than anything so far in my life. And I got it. I should be happy.

And all smiles I was.

At least... until I arrived home.

b l a c k e

Sometime during the day, nobody really knowing why or how, Smokey had gotten out.

The back gate was swung open. My mom swears she never went back there or never saw anyone, for that matter. And I never blamed her. My dad didn't get home on that day until after me. But there he was, my beloved Golden Retriever, lying in the street amidst a pool of his own blood.

Smokey had gotten out—escaped—one way or another. The details don't always seem important when death is on the line. He had been hit by a passing car; the poor dog never had a chance because everyone in the neighborhood seemed to be either at work, school, or too busy to notice. My mom claimed she was taking a hot bath, and didn't see the tragedy, until Smokey was already a goner.

Of course I wasn't pleased with my favorite animal's death. I mourned the loss of my dog plenty. I grieved like any other, normal, child. You might think this would put a stain—a curse—on my baseball card. A scar that would only lead to memories of my fallen canine friend. But it didn't.

Secretly, I was as happy as ever. I was able to block out

the unfortunate events in life and only see my great triumphs, or in this case, my coincidental fate. It was something I carried with me my entire life.

I never questioned any correlation between the two events. Who would? Even as a child, the thought of me wishing for a special baseball card leading to my favorite Golden Retriever's death was absurd. It didn't make sense.

It was strictly a case of mere coincidence. An act of good luck and then an act of bad luck. One hand feeds the other.

Nothing more, nothing less.

O

M

<u>chapter three</u>

Morton Blacke's streak of restless nights without any sleep was now three days running.

The ending to *All Roads Lead to Damascus*... nonexistent. A proclaimed masterpiece couldn't end with a whimper, only T.S. Eliot might disagree. It needed to finish strong; it needed to be never forgotten—standing the test of time. He had brainstormed every possible scenario—happy or sad, fulfilling or leaving more, simple or stunning. Each new open door led to another day... another night... of problem-solving and endless questions. *If I do this, then I have to change that, right? How will that make the reader feel, after all these pages? Is this new twist consistent with the entire story? Is any of this even believable after another deviation?*

"Don't force it," the words break the silence. Words Mr. Blacke had spoken at least once on every bestselling novel of his. They were words of wisdom, and they could serve as any author's best friend, helping them to be patient and not succumb to mediocre storytelling.

He leaves the master bedroom, tired of the morning light casting new shadows. There are no more answers in this room. He heads downstairs, quickly bypassing the 'Great Passageway,' sidetracking himself in the west wing as he allows his thoughts to brain.

He travels about halfway down the hallway, glancing at a photo of himself on the front page of a *Chicago Tribune* feature. He sees a much younger version of himself, with thicker hair and less body fat, but he hasn't changed much. The article discusses his winning of some writer's award for fiction of the year, something he'd received for his novel, *The Surrounding Sounds*, an eerie horror tale that didn't follow the genre's typical guidelines.

He knows what he has to do. Or at least, what he should do, to find the magical ending. He needs a spark to light the match-tipped ends of his writing fingers. And then, and only then, would they bang the keys once more, chiming that glorious rat-a-tat-tat on his antique typewriter.

He turns and proceeds through the door at the end of the hallway, traveling back into the mansion's foyer. So spacious, making a person lacking confidence feel overwhelmed. He looks up at the domed ceiling, searching the high walls—lined with red, crushed velvet drapes—for answers. He then searches the part of the ceiling—dropped down with the second floor above it—closer to the white double doors that hide the dining room.

"There's nothing up there," Mr. Blacke says, followed by a long gasp of disgust. "I guess it's time to head to town."

After all, it had only been over two years.

b l a c k e

Mr. Blacke laughs at the dust that has collected on his 2004 BMW. The metallic silver paint now hides, showing itself as a dull charcoal. The light filters through horizontal windows, revealing an infinite amount of sinus-flaring particles floating in the dense air.

Parked beside his favorite automobile are two more, dirt-coated vehicles. One, a red Ferrari, that had been his wife's. And the other, a black Hummer, one of his own personal off-road toys. It wasn't the newer, H2 or H3, smaller and far less menacing, cars for pussies. It was the real thing—the old school, bad-boy gas guzzler with customized duel pipes and twenty-inch blades. When the black rims were polished, they shined like a clear night sky with sparkling stars dotting the alloy.

But all three vehicles had been stationary in Mr.

Blacke's garage on the outside of the east wing. They hadn't moved, or been to town since he had. He didn't even know if they still ran. *I'm sure one of them does...*

Mr. Blacke laughs again. He's nervous, excited, and finally able to relax, all at the same time. The numerous sensations bounce at him, all balled into one humorous emotion. The wide-ranged mixture of feelings tickle his insides; this is a big step.

Not yet fully decided on which fancy car to drive, Mr. Blacke punches the remote—the largest button—on his solid gold key chain. This particular trigger opens all three garage doors at once, allowing some fresh air to enter, and some unwelcome dust to leave.

Mr. Blacke's key chain is a large loop, with a 'B' in the center, featuring keys to all three vehicles as well as a medieval master key to the front door and a spiny skeleton key that opens all but one door in the mansion. *That* door requires a different, hidden key.

"Ahhh... fresh air. My favorite." A hint of sarcasm leaves Mr. Blacke's mouth. He prefers the indoors, locked away in his nightly chamber with a world of writing before him. But occasionally, the outdoors could really alleviate the peculiar thoughts that rushed him.

He contemplates over which automobile to take. He

doesn't know if the decision is really that difficult; or, if he is just stalling. Maybe he is bluffing. Maybe he isn't really going to town after all.

But Morton Blacke leaves the choice to chance. In his head, he marks the cars from left to right as number one, number two, and number three. After pulling a small, black notepad from his Armani shirt, and an engraved pen from his back pocket, Mr. Blacke jots down the three numbers. He then tears them from the page, trying his best to make sure their sizes are almost equal. He then folds the papers. He walks a few feet to the worktable, dropping the three choices into an empty, metal bin.

Mr. Blacke, remaining impartial and being completely fair, closes his eyes and reaches into the prizeholder. He pulls one paper out, unfolds it, and raises it closer to his face. *Car number two it is...*

Sierra Blacke's red Ferrari's motor roars in the three-quarter closed room. Morton Blacke revs the engine, the loud noise drowning out bitter memories. He hopes.

The red fireball zooms down Route 163. Mr. Blacke always thought it should be called "Loop 163." But what did he know? It only circles the five towns in the area, including Lago Diablo, which lies inside Route 163 via Exit 13.

There isn't much traffic on the highway this morning.

Blacke cruises, tinted windows down, allowing his black hair to flow freely. Dark shades hide his nervous yellow eyes. He taps his fingers against the pink steering wheel cover (his wife's favorite color; his was ironically black), humming to the beat of an unknown melody playing from the car's CD player. It was the last CD Sierra had listened to before her death. And the last CD that *he* had... well... forget it. Mr. Blacke felt he was paying her some sort of homage—honoring her with this musical choice.

He hammers down on the accelerator. He didn't give a shit about the "do-riders," a cop name used often by his grandmother when he was a young lad, mostly because he had plenty of money to pay for a laughable speeding ticket.

A drop of water bounces off his left elbow, which is partially hanging out the Ferrari's open window. A few more drops splash against the front glass. Then steady rain begins to come down. It is the third time this week it's rained. And Mr. Blacke is forced to remove the "cool" from his long overdue trip to town and roll up the windows.

"Ridiculous," Mr. Blacke says, turning the music down to a low background noise. The words are spoken based on the fact that it was raining, yet the sun remained shining. There were scattered clouds across the velvety sky, but the golden round heater found a gap and held true. *I'll have to remember to use this in my book—something like, 'it was bizarre, almost as strange as rain falling with the sun out.'*

Mr. Blacke likes the sentence. He opens the car's mid-console, finding a fountain pen and a pink notepad. He also sees a picture of him and Sierra, but closes the lid on the console before it takes a real shape—a real form in his mind. He uses the pen, chicken-scratching down his ideas while simultaneously taking Exit 13 toward Lago Diablo.

Blacke stops at the red light before turning left on Lakeside Boulevard—the street that takes you right into the downtown area. It is about three more miles to town; but first, you have to pass over the Laughing Bridge, which spans the one-mile lake the town is named for. He watches as boats zip up and down the midnight-blue water, leaving streaks of white behind them. There are some fishermen on the peers and alongside the lake, not allowing the morning drizzle to spoil their favorite hobby. Mr. Blacke sees one exceptionally large and fancy yacht, appearing to have a small group aboard. He looks at his silver and gold Rolex—9:37 a.m.—and thinks that these lake-goers might be jumping the gun on their weekend, being it only Friday.

Mr. Blacke lets off the gas as the town of Lago Diablo is in sight. Speeding on an open highway is one thing, but reckless driving where children and pedestrians are is quite different. He passes the Lago State Bank on his left and puts on his blinker. He parks in front of the Lago Food Mart, curious whether or not they have any fresh rock lobster.

The rain has stopped for the moment, dark stains of recent moisture soak the asphalt. Before Morton Blacke can even get completely out of his wife's red Ferrari, he is greeted by the store's owner—the man who also owns the Lago Diner.

"Oh, my, Mr. Blacke," Doug St. Clair begins, carrying a bag of deer corn in his arms. Doug is wearing a faded red tee and shorts that are way too short, showing his awful white tan line around the knee and lower thigh. He has the slightest bit of panic in his voice. He is obviously very surprised to see the famous author. "I'm so sorry, did Arnold or... umm... Paul... forget your delivery this week?"

"No, Doug." Mr. Blacke fully stands outside the low car. "Everything is fine."

"Oh, that's wonderful! What brings you to town? It's been awhile, hasn't it? Or not that long, really." The store owner's words are quick to exit his twitching mouth and appear to be an attempt at prying, but trying to be polite in doing so.

"Only two years, Doug," Mr. Blacke says, flashing a comical smile. "Hell... seems like just yesterday I was having a piece of that fantastic pecan pie next door."

"It sure does," Doug says, unsure of how he really feels about his answer. He scratches his head with his free hand, shifting the few brown hairs that are still sticking to his scalp. They are darker due to the dampness in the air. Mr. Blacke guesses he had been out in the light rain. Doug St. Clair stands in front of Lago Diablo's ghost writer (almost literally), still holding the bag of feed.

"That bag looks heavy," Mr. Blacke says, patting Doug on the shoulder and heading for the Lago Food Mart's front door. Morton turns around before going in and says, "You should have someone else carry it."

But Mr. Blacke doesn't offer. He meant... someone other than himself. He doesn't wait for an answer as he allows the door with the single-pane window to close gently behind him. He hears Doug say something like 'it's not that bad' simultaneous to the grocery store's greeting bell above the doorway. Mr. Blacke draws curious eyes from a young—probably high school age—blonde-haired girl behind the store's first register. There are only two checkout spots in the Lago Food Mart and only one is currently open. An elderly, gray-haired man, sporting a rustic-bronze cane, also stares at the forgotten author from the checkout aisle. He has only a few items to purchase, but when Mr. Blacke walks in, everything comes to a halt.

Blondie says hello, followed by a nod from the old man. Mr. Blacke isn't sure whether they are trying not to be nosy, or whether they truly don't know who he is. Either way, he's happy with the present situation. He gives the twosome a brief salute, saying 'hi' beneath his breath. He passes them, smiling at the sight of a deep red spaghetti stain on the man's button-down shirt. *A little early for Italian, isn't it?*

He heads through the produce section towards the back of the store. He passes a woman in her mid-forties, a little weathered and chapped from the summer dry winds of the area, who gives him a double-take, but doesn't approach him or stop him on his quest for fresh seafood.

So far, so good.

Mr. Blacke begins to think that taking a trip to town isn't so bad after all. He nestles up to the meat counter, having to draw close to see through the foggy glass viewing area. He first sees an assortment of steaks—ribeye's, t-bones, filet's, etc. His eyes scan further along, passing up the fresh-cut pork chops and tenderloins and chicken breasts, and finally coming to the seafood section of the display.

There are fresh, deep sea Tiger shrimp, scallions, raw oysters, snow crab, and the rock lobster he has had his heart set on. The sound of a machine cutting steaks blares in the back of the butcher area. Mr. Blacke glares at the lobsters, trying to find the two perfect ones that would love to take a swim in a pot of boiling water. The sound ceases. The man with a bloodied apron and latex gloves looks up and sees his customer.

He begins, "How can I help you, sir—" but as he draws closer, he recognizes the writer. "Hey! Mr. Blacke! How ya' been? We missed you and your witty jokes back here."

"Things are good, Philly." The butcher, Philip Embers, was just as big a Sopranos fan as was Pete Vincenzo. Except Philip, had no Italian blood beneath his pale white skin. He had all of his workers calling him 'Philly,' after Frank Vincent's character. Morton Blacke sees another worker moving around by the back freezer.

"Hey Paulie, look who's here!" Philip calls to Paul Diego, one of Mr. Blacke's frequent delivery boys. The 'Paulie' reference is accented with Philip Embers best Italian; and it could go either way—Sopranos or Godfather. "Come say hello to Mr. Blacke."

Paul walks up to the counter, standing next to the head butcher. Philip Embers jabs Paulie in the ribs, but the twenty-year old boy ignores the friendly blow. "How's it goin', Mr. Blacke? I didn't forget anything, did I?"

"No Paul, everything's perfect," Mr. Blacke says, patiently waiting to order his favorite seafood. And then another person interrupts the three, joining in with the greetings.

"Mr. Blacke, sir. It's very nice to see you again."

Morton Blacke turns behind him. He sees a familiar fellow, short, near-bald, with perfectly-rimmed glasses. The man's hand is already extended towards him. Mr. Blacke raises his own hand, saying, "It's nice to see you again, too, mister... mister—"

"Spencer," the man adds, shaking Mr. Blacke's hand. "Ray Spencer. The reporter from the *Lago Diablo News*."

"I knew that," Mr. Blacke says, smiling and turning back to face the butcher. "I was just testing you... making sure you knew."

Both Mr. Blacke and Philly laugh. The reporter seems confused for a few seconds, but then joins in as if it was the greatest joke ever told. Mr. Blacke doesn't turn back around. Instead, he rolls his eyes at the butcher, hoping the little man will move along. Ray Spencer does just that. The reporter says farewell, Mr. Blacke gives a quick wave, and a second interview is avoided.

"That was a close one," Mr. Blacke tells Philly.

"Yeah, no shit. Fuckin' reporters."

Morton Blacke responds with a slight grin. He then motions for the butcher to follow his eyes—his moving fingers. The author from the 'Mansion on the Hill' points at one lobster, saying 'that one,' and then to a second lobster, saying 'and also that one.'

"Nice choices, Mr. Blacke. Couldn't have picked a better pair myself."

"That's why you weren't doing the picking," Mr. Blacke says, a silly smirk drawn across his face.

"Neverending," Philly responds. He wraps the two rock lobsters and begins to weigh them. "You know, it's been over two years... I believe... and it seems like just yesterday you were in here bustin' my chops."

"Pork?"

"Ahh... enough of that shit. I'm going to keep my mouth shut." Philly marks down the price with a black-tipped crayon and hands the package to his customer. "You have a wonderful day, Mr. Blacke."

"You too, Philly." Morton Blacke heads back towards the register, taking a detour to view the selections in the alcoholic-beverage aisle. As soon as he turns the corner, eyes ready to scan along the stacked shelves, something else catches his attention. It's a woman.

The gorgeous brunette, with layered hair tumbling just

past her exposed shoulders, is holding a bottle of wine in one hand and carrying one of the Lago Food Mart blue shopping baskets in the other. From Morton Blacke's view, the sides of her rosy cheeks look gentle and refreshingly smooth. Her long, tanned legs glow beneath a checkered brown and yellow skirt. Her cutoff white blouse is tucked in; the top button undone, revealing just enough to arouse a passer's curiosity, but not suspect anything sleazy.

Now Mr. Blacke doesn't have any intentions. He is just being the friendly character, witty and sarcastic, that the town used to love dearly. He walks right up behind the pretty woman, slightly leaning over her shoulder. He doesn't get close enough to be creepy or invade her space. But very subtle like, he glances at the bottle of wine she's holding—*Kendall Jackson Merlot, 2004.*

"That one's good, but I prefer this one," Morton Blacke startles the woman from her decision-making. She moves slightly, faces him, and warms to his soothing voice with a picturesque smile. Her turquoise eyes greet his—beams of immediate romance travel to and fro amidst the fine rails of the parallel invisible.

Mr. Blacke signals for her to give him one second. He walks down the aisle a few feet and reaches for the top shelf. He grabs a bottle of *Napa Valley Silver Oak, 2003.* He brings the bottle back to the woman, holding it before her like someone presenting a prestigious award. She smiles.

He says, "I've had more expensive wine, but this one is by far the best bang for your buck."

"That one is still a little beyond my budget," the woman says, still smiling while shrugging her shoulders in a friendly manner.

"Nonsense," Mr. Blacke says. "How about... if you really want a bottle of fine wine for the evening, this one's on me."

"I couldn't let you do that," the woman quickly responds to his kind gesture.

"Nonsense again. It would be my pleasure. The name is Morton Blacke." He wisely holds out his left hand, trying to ease the handshaking situation as the woman has her basket in the traditional shaking hand.

"Yeah... I know. I've been trying to pretend I'm not completely overwhelmed. I just finished your book, *The Surrounding Sounds*. Umm... it was recommended by a friend here in town. And *it* was very good." The brunette appears to be getting slightly nervous, as she has trouble placing the wine bottle back on the shelf without dropping it. She turns to Morton Blacke, who is calmly waiting for her hand, and shakes. "My name is Leslie Vitter. And I just moved to Lago

Diablo about a month ago."

"Well... it's my treat to be in your presence, Miss Vitter. And thank you for the kind feedback." Mr. Blacke quickly searches for a ring with clever eyes, but sees no signs of marriage.

"Your treat?" Leslie Vitter asks, raising her perfectly-plucked eyebrows. "I assure you, the treat is all mine."

"Have it your way," Morton Blacke says. "Now about that bottle of wine... will you take me up on my offer?"

"On one condition..." Leslie responds, smiling and waiting for the famous writer's response.

"And what might that be?" Morton takes the bait.

"If you help me drink it." As soon as the words exit the beautiful woman's mouth, her confidence growing with every line, partially because of the ease in socializing with Morton Blacke, Leslie Vitter remembers that the author had recently lost his wife. This is all too familiar to her. It stings her on a personal level... and the irony is quite 'sarcastically amusing.' Regarding Morton's situation, she didn't realize it had been two years since his wife's passing. So she quickly adds, "I'm so sorry if I seemed too forward. I shouldn't be so pushy."

"Of course not," Mr. Blacke says, relaxing the situation. But he doesn't answer her question. Leslie doesn't know whether to just take him up on the *Silver Oak* offer and forget about her condition, or to pursue further. She chooses to simply drop the invite for the time being.

The new acquaintances walk down the aisle, back towards the front registers. Before arriving at the blonde girl's lane, Morton asks, "Finished shopping?"

"Yes, I was. Thank you." The woman begins unloading her few groceries from the shopping basket—eggs, cottage cheese, strawberries, plums, pomegranate juice, and some frozen chicken breasts. Morton places the bottle of wine amongst her groceries, along with his two rock lobsters. The woman gives him a brief, puzzled look, but doesn't say anything. She waits to see what is going to unfold.

"All together?" the girl asks, reaching for the nearest item.

"Yes," Morton says, moving in front of Leslie. She looks at him with big eyes, seeming to say that his generosity isn't necessary. Morton responds to her reaction, whispering "Please... don't worry 'bout it."

"Thank you so much, Mr. Blacke," Leslie says in a soft voice.

"Call me Morton." He reaches for his black, ostrich wallet. He pulls a couple of hundred-dollar bills from inside and gently tosses them down on the counter. The young girl displays the total for him to see—$178.46. She bags the groceries together before getting the author his change.

"That's not necessary," Mr. Blacke says before she begins to count money. "Keep it. Buy yourself a nice dinner."

The blonde girl smiles from ear to ear. "Thank you so much, Mr. Blacke."

She knows who I am after all...

Morton carries all the groceries outside, happy to be leaving that ringing bell behind. Leslie follows behind him, still uncertain of what's unfolding. Once outside, the rains leaving for today, Morton adjusts his eyes to extreme sunlight. He squints and waits a few seconds. He then turns to the brunette in her early thirties, and says, "My place or yours?"

At first, Leslie is caught off guard. She is unsure of the question he is asking. She has completely forgotten her earlier invitation to drink together.

"Also," Morton proceeds before she can respond. "Do you like lobster?"

Leslie gently laughs, not losing control, but just hard enough for Morton to see another attractive and friendly side of his new friend. "Yes... I love lobster! Who doesn't? And we can try my place, since I invited *you* and all."

"Works for me." Morton places the bags of groceries in

the back of her white Lincoln Aviator, which is parked in the same line as his Ferrari, but just across the street. "I'll follow you."

He walks back to his car, giving the woman a friendly wave. Right before he can duck down in his wife's red speeder, another prying character shouts at him. "Morton! Morton! Wait a second!"

He raises his head, mid-dip into the car, and peers in the direction of the downtown sidewalk passing before several storefronts. *Goddammit!* Morton recognizes the lumpy man in his fifties, with a slick comb over and bushy brows. The charging man's name is Robert Goodlew. He is a fellow author, though less famous. Actually... he's not famous at all. He was self-published about five years ago and believes to be in some sort of club with Morton—a distinguished bond between writers, giving him a special pass to talk to Morton about anything regarding his work, no matter the time or day. No matter that it has been over two years since Morton's last trip to Lago Diablo.

"Morton! Wait up!" Robert Goodlew shouts, now breathing heavily because he had to do more than just walk.

"Goddammit," Morton says beneath his breath. Only the cracked asphalt, a lighter, shale shade now where the post-rain sun has kissed it, hears his comical disgust at not getting away in time. *Maybe the trip to town wasn't a good idea after all...* Then Morton remembers Leslie and quickly tosses the thought aside like a crumpled piece of paper. A little louder, with a false face, Morton asks, "How's the writing, Robert?"

The man bends over, grabbing his knees. He wipes sweat from his wrinkled brow with an unwashed handkerchief. Leslie now backs out of her parking spot into the middle of the street. She stops the vehicle, looking back to see if Morton is ready to follow her. The famous author turns towards Leslie's vehicle. With an amusing grimace on his face, he motions for her to wait. Meanwhile, Robert Goodlew has finally recovered from his goofy trot to catch his self-proclaimed colleague.

"Morton, it's so great to see you." Robert is one of the few people who calls Mr. Blacke by his first name. Normally, Morton wouldn't mind one ounce, but because of his irritated feelings toward this bothersome character, the first-name bit rubs him the wrong way. "I've been wanting to get your opinion on this new fiction war story I'm working on. I've got over three-hundred pages as is. I even came by your house up on the hill a few times, but you must not have been home."

Oh... I was home alright. Idiot.

"That's fantastic, Bob." Morton decides he would try the first-name thing again, but this time with a little twist. "When I have some free time, I will get a hold of you and see what I can do. Right now, though, I've got to run. Time is of the essence."

"Thanks, Morton," Robert says, stepping closer to the vehicle. "But are you sure—"

"Gotta' jet, Bob," Morton interrupts, crawling into the Ferrari. Before closing the door, he adds. "I'll catch up with you next time."

The door slams as Robert Goodlew accepts his fate and says a friendly farewell. Morton Blacke backs out of the Lago Food Mart's front row parking and thinks...

Wish I would've gotten a piece of pecan pie...

Maybe tomorrow?

b l a c k e

Mr. Blacke pulls his wife's red Ferrari alongside the front of the house on Misty Lane.

The neighborhood isn't filthy rich, but everyone here seems to have a nice share of change, and they usually keep their quaint homes eye-pleasing with exotic, well-groomed plants and fresh paint. Leslie's domain appears to be one of these.

The yard has been recently mowed and the narrow sidewalk leading to the small patio has been neatly scalped with the works of a gas-powered weedeater. Each window on the front side of the house features decorative blue shutters, with hand-painted yellow flowers dotted, evenly spaced. The cozy home is constructed of an orange-tan brick, not too flashy or gaudy.

Mr. Blacke exits his car, following the cement towards the front door, located on the right side of the house. Leslie waits by the door with the two bags of groceries, cycling her set of keys for the magical one. As Mr. Blacke reaches the covered porch, he dodges several spiny plants, hanging out of the sides of rich-soiled terracotta pots guarding the entrance.

"Here... let me help with those," Mr. Blacke offers, extending a hand to her side.

"Oh, thanks." Leslie hands over the bags, still shuffling trying to find the right key. With another free hand, the process becomes much easier. She locates the winner, sticks it in the top lock, and slides the inner bolt away from its locking position.

She opens the door and moves inside, turning to

motion Morton to follow. He enters behind her, still without any preordained intentions or motives besides the urge to have lobster and wine with someone other than himself—a new friend.

Mr. Blacke searches the living area, agreeing with her taste on the choices of colors and furniture within the merlot-painted walls. Her main sitting piece, a beige-cushioned loveseat with natural-wood arms, lies in the center. It faces a stone mantle, the finishing touch above a three-foot gray hearth and a few, unburned logs resting in the fireplace. *I don't remember seeing a chimney? Must have missed it...* A deep red, rectangular rug, with blotches of yellow and peach, cover nearly all of the hardwood floor. Besides a couple of paintings on the walls, a replica Van Gogh above the mantle, the only other thing that catches Mr. Blacke's eye is a light brown reading chair, with a copy of *The Surrounding Sounds* resting adjacent to it on top of a black metal stand—circular crest.

"The living room is very nice," Mr. Blacke says as Leslie Vitter leads him through an opening on the opposite wall of the front door, proceeding to the kitchen. There is one other cutout on the fourth wall, which appears to lead to bedrooms and bathrooms.

"I'm glad you like it. Thanks."

The kitchen is a little crowded for Morton's liking, but still well-organized and decorated. The dining table, made of some darker wood, is capped off nicely by an antique, wiry centerpiece candle-holder that stands a couple of feet high. It features five different layers to place candles—the ones already aboard release scents of vanilla and cinnamon. Nothing too adventurous... nothing too bold.

The dining area feeds right into the cooking area, both rooms painted with a creamy white. The cabinets and counters match the coffee-colored table, as if they were composed of the exact same tree. The appliances are older models, but have had proper upkeep and fit the design.

"Where do you want these?" Morton asks, holding the grocery bags a little higher.

"You can set them right there." Leslie points to a spot on the counter nearest the white-porcelain sink. She opens a drawer next to the fridge and pulls out a sterling silver corkscrew. She walks over to Morton, standing along the counter on his immediate left. "You ready for a glass?"

Her eyes meet his... and then quickly glance down, focusing on the bottle of *Silver Oak*. Morton grabs the bottle, handing it over.

"Sure," he says with a confident smile. "Let's open this bad boy up and let it breathe a little."

While Leslie pulls the cork from the wine bottle, Morton begins opening the wrapped rock lobsters. She tugs hard, the *plop* sound that follows almost causes her to lose her balance, but she stabilizes herself against the countertop. Leslie laughs. Morton smiles, raising his eyebrows in a friendly, playful manner.

"I got it under control," she says, setting the bottle down by the sink. She walks to the end of the counter, closer to the dining table and passing Morton along the way. She opens the above cabinet, reaching up to one of the higher shelves to gather two wine glasses. She turns back to her new "author" friend. She laughs again. This time, shaking her head with simple amusement.

"What's so funny?" Morton asks, holding up one of the lobsters and playing the puppet-master before her eyes. They share polite smiles. And then Leslie answers.

"I dunno. It's just a little weird, that's all."

"I'm not following."

"I mean... come on. A world-famous author, Morton Blacke, here in my humble home." For the first time since Morton met her, she shows a lack of confidence that is expected. After all, he didn't really know her background, but *his* name appeared day and night in newspapers, magazines, bookstores, right along with his handsome face.

The book she just finished, *The Surrounding Sounds*, reached number one on the bestseller's list worldwide. For Leslie, a woman in her thirties and almost ten years younger than her new friend, to be slightly intimidated or feel she'd been swept away into a dream world, is completely understandable. Leslie finishes, "It's surreal. I'm honored and very, very flattered."

"Trust me," Morton begins, taking a step closer to her. "I'm the one who should be flattered. In the presence of such pure beauty and obvious intellect."

Leslie blushes as Morton reaches for the wine glasses. He takes them from her hands with a gentle touch. He says, "Now we've got something to drink to."

She laughs in agreement as he pours the smooth, deep red wine into the glasses. He hands one to Leslie, raising his next to hers. Morton toasts, "To a wonderful new friend... and to a pleasant evening of lobster and fine conversation."

Leslie nods. The poetic *ding* of colliding glasses follows. She looks into his eyes as they both indulge in the room-temperature *Silver Oak*. Her eyes widen and her smile broadens. She nods a second time, this time in approval for the silky smooth wine.

"It's terrific," she says, sipping a second offering. "And you, Morton Blacke, are simply amazing." And she means this—the way the words flow from his mouth without any sign of nervousness or without any notion that he is ever unsure of himself.

He shrugs and grins. He returns to the lobsters. "Got a pot?"

"Of course. Let me tend to that, please."

"No no. I'll handle it just fine, thank you. I just need a pot, some of your finest seasoning, and some plates."

"I think I can arrange that," Leslie says. She directs Morton to the necessary tools, and then proceeds to unpack and refrigerate the rest of the groceries that sit atop the dark wood counter. "Do you want anything specific for sides?"

Morton acts as though he is in deep thought. He then answers, "Nope. Lobster's all I need."

Leslie rolls her eyes with a friendly demeanor. She feels as though they've been friends for a long time. Her early comfort and ease at being around him is surprising, especially since she hadn't been with anyone since...

"Are you sure?" she asks a second time, opening the fridge.

"I'm just playing around," Morton says, filling the large cooking pot with warm water. He places it on the stove, turning the burner to high. "Whatever you want is perfectly fine with me."

"How 'bout a potato? I have a few toppings."

"That would be great," Morton says, lightly salting the water. "Lemons?"

"For the potatoes?" Leslie asks, peering into the refrigerator's bottom shelves.

"No, silly. For the boiling water and lobsters." Morton makes a comical face—mouth agape—at her as she looks up from behind the open fridge door. She laughs at his expression, turning back around to grab a fresh lemon. "Also... some butter would be nice."

"Okay, okay. Don't rush me." The words have no trace of irritation within them. They are playful and full of a relaxing glee that had previously been missing from Leslie Vitter's life. Missing for quite some time now. Missing since...

"Can you watch the water for me?" Morton asks. "I need to use the men's room."

Leslie brings his requested supplies and sets them down on open counter space besides the stovetop. "Sure, no problem," she responds.

"I believe I could find it," Morton begins to say while heading back towards the living room. "But I thought it might be polite to ask."

"Oh yeah, silly me." Leslie taps the side of her head

with her fingers. "Go through the other opening in the living room and it's your first door on the left."

"Thanks," Morton says, leaving the kitchen.

As he enters the small hallway, featuring three doors; the first, leading to his destination bath, while the second and third, he guesses are bedrooms (master and guest), Morton reflects upon the unfolding situation before him.

He misses Sierra. At least, the wife he knew in the beginning. But as always, he shoves that bitter memory aside, pushing it behind some dusty, cobweb-covered boxes in back corner of his mind. He thinks on the present events. This beautiful woman, Leslie, with such welcoming eyes and a smile that he couldn't get out of his head, did she deserve him?

Please don't misunderstand Mr. Blacke... don't misinterpret his question one bit. He isn't asking out of conceitedness or implying that he is too good for her. He is worried. He is cautious. He doesn't want his past to continue with its "normal" dire calamities that seem to epilogue his great successes. This, my friend—this incredible person wanting to share a night of lobster and wine and perhaps the beginning of a fond friendship or a little romance—is the main reason Mr. Blacke hadn't left his home in some time.

But he needed help. Selfishly? That's for you to decide.

He needed an ending to cap off the masterful... the epic, *All Roads Lead to Damascus*. And for this, he ventured out. He defied his own logic and words of wariness. *Maybe this time things will be different...*

The reaching hope is nothing more than simple lies to hide his grief in an empty heart chamber bound—

Something hanging in the hallway diverts his wandering mind. He sees a picture of Leslie, with a man, kissing. He sees another one of her with this man. And then he sees another one, this one is the icing on the cake with wedding gown and wedding tux. Mr. Blacke is confused. Sometimes, people eagerly want answers to clear their scattered thoughts, but going about in getting those answers isn't always that easy.

He shakes his head—an imaginary eraser sweeps across his brain and provides Mr. Blacke with a clean slate. He opens the first door and heads into the bathroom.

b l a c k e

"How's the fresh lobster?" Morton asks, forking another buttery bite.

"It's superb," Leslie answers. "I haven't had any in

what seems like ages. Maybe the last time was at the shore with..." The beautiful woman trails off, swiping at her brow. She picks up her white-silk napkin and dabs at her eyes. "I'm sorry." The words are spoken downward—spoken to the recently laid-out table cloth.

"Did I-I... say something wrong?" A slight stutter as the words leave Morton's mouth for the first time, not so smooth. He sets his glass of wine down and pushes back against his chair, sliding away from one end of the dining table. He rises, moving towards Leslie, not exactly sure what to do next. She gathers herself and speaks.

"No, not at all. Umm... I'm sorry. I don't know what's come over me. I really should explain a few things to you." Morton touches Leslie's shoulder with a familiar consoling hand. She looks up at him and forces a smile—her inside telling her it's right, her outside not wanting to feel so festive.

"Whatever you feel is best," Morton says patiently. "Trust me, I know all too well the misfortunes of life."

Leslie giggles, holding her damp napkin in one hand and pressing against her soft, yet flat stomach with the other. Morton doesn't fully understand her reaction, but he hopes Leslie will clarify. And she does.

"*Trust me,*" Leslie Vitter, formerly Leslie Ferguson, says

with a 'there's more behind it than you know' smirk on her face—full lips pressed together. She continues, "You know them better than you think, Morton."

Mr. Blacke says nothing. He stands beside her, listening with a rising curiosity.

Leslie Vitter fills him in. "To keep it short and sweet, and not, umm... bring up too many painful memories, I'll just throw it out there. We. Both. Have lost our spouses in car wrecks."

The words are shocking. Morton Blacke licks the bottom of his lip, before softly biting into it. His teeth do not clench down hard enough to draw blood, but he feels a slight sensation of discomfort. He can't think of anything to say. He does, however, think of something not to say. *I wonder if her dead husband was cheating on her during his fatal crash?*

"I just felt that you should know. My husband died three years ago... next month that is. He was killed when a teenager flew through an intersection going eighty, ignoring the stop sign." She pauses to gather herself. Morton rubs the top of her back, his fingers gliding through her brown hair. Leslie adds, "Especially... since I've read about your tragic events in life, I thought you should know about mine."

Silence fills the fresh seafood-aroma dining area. The

warm dipping butter, along with the lobsters and potatoes, begin to cool. Morton leans down, touching her chin with his index finger and thumb, and gently lifts. Her dark mascara, applied just light enough to enhance beauty rather than appear gothic or overbearing, is beginning to smear. Although, her moist eyes retain the sentimental allure that first intrigued Morton Blacke.

"Well... at least we have something in common," Morton says with a caring smile. Leslie shakes her head and returns the pleasing expression. They share a moment, one entangled with vines of scarred pasts and sorrowful recollections. If one can't find humor in irony, then one might as well not exist.

"I suppose we have that," Leslie says, rising from the table. And with arms open, "I could use a hug."

Morton concurs. He embraces her, just close enough to be romantic, but not close enough to be pervertedly creepy. No scoop and lift, just a warming embrace. After, Morton asks, "Shall we finish dinner?"

The couple of damaged friends return to their original seating. They are finished with their painful pasts for tonight. Instead, they share childhood stories, they share similar interests and hobbies, they share personal preferences on books, music, movies, and most of all, they share a special bond—a bond that each believe they felt... they saw... earlier in the day at the Lago Food Mart.

O

R

M

chapter four

It had been eight years since the death of Smokey.

I was in my third year of college, attending Johns Hopkins University. Things were at a bedlam. The rush of my growing fame was exciting, dreamlike, and sometimes slightly demanding. There weren't too many authors who climbed the bestseller's list before they could even have a legal drink.

Everything was happening very quickly. Between classes, and studying, I attended scheduled book signings and readings. My first novel, *Every Dog Has Its Night*—insert pun here—was well-received by a wide variety of literary crowds. It was picked up by Random House despite being an unagented submission. I must have hit the jackpot. Copies of the book had been mailed out in every direction, from *Publisher's Weekly* to *Kirkus* to the *Library Journal*, searching for some prestigious reviews. And the unbelievable praise seemed unending.

The *San Jose Mercury News* said, "Blacke's mesmerizing

writing is unlike any of his chasing generation." The *New York Times* said, "*Every Dog Has Its Night* sets the bar for fiction writing." And the *USA Today* said, "Every half-century or so, a writer takes the bestseller's list by storm, this is the time of Blacke."

These were just a few of the good reviews. Like I stated, they just kept on coming and the book sales just kept on soaring—the way an eagle climbs after snagging a scrumptious snack. I was in awe. But somewhere, deep down in the lower cavern of my self-proclaimed hollow body, a light was on. The light—

It spoke of all-knowing. It flashed a greater understanding for the success that I was being introduced. It said, 'Morty,' in a voice scarily similar to my father's, but one easily recognized as a figment of my creative mind, 'you knew this book was going to be a hit. You knew it was going to be one-of-a-kind. You knew it was going to be your breakthrough into the writing world—an author who would soon be sought out by every high-ranking literary agent and top-of-the-line publishing house in the modern world.'

I smiled at the accusations. That famous, delightfully devilish pose that would be captured in newspaper photo after magazine photo after free press photo in years to come. The beckoning light finished, 'Morty, you knew it was going to set you on the one-track rails of stardom for the rest of your life. And with all this, you knew it was going to cost that... that... that...'

The antique record player began to skip. The dusty black arm snagged on an unseen bump protruding a millimeter higher than the rest of the large disc. The record playing... maybe Led Zeppelin, maybe The Who, or maybe even some Dire Straits.

"... And with all this, you damn well knew it was going to cost that—"

That poor boy his...

The light tried to shine through the heavy fog that lingered inside me, but it couldn't reach the outers. It was being suffocated like hanging venison in a smokehouse. It couldn't keep me from my success. It attempted to reveal something—someone—more, behind the curtain like the Master Oz; it just really wasn't me.

I was still the young boy that loved Dwight Evans. I was still the teenager who loved the smell of a baseball diamond. I was still the little kid sharing late-night stories that I had made up in my head with my best friends.

I pleaded the "bad luck" slash "ill fate" slash "mere coincidence" card once again.

b l a c k e

Jeffrey Jane had spent an all-niter at the Johns Hopkins University Library, studying his ass off for near impossible-to-pass finals.

Every hour or so, he would take a fifteen-minute break to read his roommate's, his best college friend's, novel that was taking the nation by storm. *Advanced Physics* on his bottom left, *British Literature* on his left, but stacked one layer higher, *Mechanical Engineering* directly in front of him, and *Every Dog Has Its Night* taunting on his right.

Jeffrey, growing tired of looking up and seeing that traditional, glassed-in white library clock staring back at him, rose from his padded red chair. He packed his books and headed towards the third-floor elevator.

He had just sloshed through a ten-hour study shift. He was proud, knowing his parents would greatly approve, yet exhausted. His mind was tired; he truly hoped that studying multiple fields of knowledge wouldn't cause all his acquired facts and new wisdom to run together like mixed paint. Of course Blake knew nothing of splitting atoms. Yeats, though a great mind, didn't create a formula for vacuum-sucking water out of deep rivers for bridge-building. And Browning most likely knew little of altering DNA chromosomes for quick-fix sex changes.

Bing, the elevator chimed. The doors mechanically slid open. Jeffery Jane entered the new age dumbwaiter—for people, and much larger transportation means rather than meals—and pressed the button for ground level.

Another beeping sound soon followed after reaching his desired floor. As the doors automatically spread open, Jeffrey couldn't help but notice a pretty blonde, working at the library's information desk. Her smile seemed to lighten the room as she chatted with two other apparent students, a guy and a girl, not nearly as eye-catching. Jeffrey contemplated walking up to her and introducing himself, but shrugged it off.

'Grow some balls,' he thought, heading for the main doors. 'I'll talk to her next time..."

If only there was a next time.

He exited the building, feeling a blast a nippy-winter air on his clean-shaved cheeks as he used an extra bit of strength to open the library's double doors. His light brown hair was just long enough to move from the wind's unpredictable gusts. He now regretted the fact that he had left his beanie on his bed, in the room next door to where I currently was trying to get some much-needed sleep.

It was an hour past midnight when Jeffrey began his nine-block stroll to our better-than-average house. His parents, much wealthier than mine, had forked up the cash for the place, paying for the deposit and a semester's worth of rent as long as we maintained a 3.5 or higher. That was the bargain... that was the deal.

Jeffrey Jane had walked home from different campus locations many days and many nights before this one. Everything seemed the same. With zombied movements, one knowing the path they travel like the back of their hand, able to do it blindfolded if need be, Jeffrey crossed Guilford Avenue, trying to keep his heavy eyes open.

He never saw the maroon-red Blazer, cruising around the neighborhood with lights off, looking for serious trouble.

b l a c k e

A late-night, early-morning phone call disturbed me from my deep slumber. I remember dreaming of sweet Annie Redmond, not too bright for a fellow Hopkins' student, but she had a pretty face to go along with her huge breasts. She was what one might call 'book smart.' She loved class participation and group projects, but common sense seemed to play 'hide-and-seek' with her brain.

Ring... ring... ring... I finally picked it up, lifting the big white banana phone from its designated landing. A voice I didn't recognize spoke on the other side.

"Is this Morton Blacke?"

Breathing heavily into the phone, I managed to get one eye open. My flashing, neon-red alarm radio signaled that it was 3:07 a.m. "Who is this?" I questioned the question.

"This is Detective Sanders with the Baltimore Police Department," the man spoke sternly, but not viciously. "Now please, if you don't mind answering my question."

"Yes, sir, officer. This is Morton Blacke."

"Are you Jeffrey Jane's roommate, son?" The detective's voice was barely above a whisper. Something felt wrong. *What did that idiot do this time?* I wondered...

"Yes, sir. I am." We shared a brief moment of silence. I didn't know if Detective Sanders was waiting on me to add something more or trying to think of what he was going to say next. The suspense was torturing me. "Is he in some sort of trouble?"

"No, son, I'm afraid not. It's a little worse than that. He's been... murdered." The last word exited the detective's mouth like it had been rehearsed and stated many times before, but each time, it was just as difficult to say.

"What?" I asked, shocked. I sat up in bed, allowing the phone to drop to the top sheet. I stared at the opposing wall—streetlights making shadowy figures, warped and twisted. *Could this be an occurrence forced by my new success? An effect to the Every Dog Has Its Night cause?* I moved the thoughts aside with a turned cheek. I reached for the phone again. I could hear the detective's voice, asking something along the lines of, 'Are you still there, Morton?'

I put the phone against my left ear. "Morton?" Detective Sanders asked again, with a concerned tone.

"I'm here," I answered. A barrage of questions swarmed my mind like bees defending their queen. "What-what happened? Uhh... how did you know to call me? Where did this happen?"

"I'm really sorry, son," the detective started. "It appears that your friend was shot by someone passing by in a vehicle. We don't have any witnesses as of yet, just speculation and the evidence. But he was shot several times. And was dead upon arrival. It happened a few blocks from your house while he was walking home, we guess."

"He was coming home from studying at the library," I said. "How did you know to call here... and me?"

"We found a copy of your novel in his backpack. It was

signed... *To Jeffrey Jane, my roommate and dear friend."*

If the situation wasn't melancholy enough, the signed copy of *my* novel found at the crime scene definitely dropped the hammer. It felt like someone had just kicked me in the middle of the stomach with a hard-toe boot. Nauseous. Gasping for air. I set the phone down on the hook. I figured the officer would call back with more questions—like did Jeffrey have any enemies? Either way, I had heard enough.

Because I was Morton Blacke. And come daylight, everything would be better. My book, *Every Dog Has Its Night*, would soon reach #1 on most of the bestsellers' lists. My fame and success would continue to grow, more than any skeptic would have ever imagined. Even Michael Shermer would have been a believer in Morton Blacke.

I didn't accept the idea that the gruesome murder was my fault. I mean, come on, think on the situation for a brief moment. It just wasn't possible. The immediate rise of my novel linked to Jeffrey Jane's death. Tell that to a religious cult, and even they would laugh in your face.

As with Smokey, it just didn't add up.

Even though, deep inside, I could feel it flowing through the reds and blues of my veins, I didn't yet want to admit it. One time, nothing more than a sordid coincidence.

Two times, not enough to develop a pattern, just a twisted misfortune.

But three times? Four times?

I didn't know that it was going to cost that poor boy his life.

T
R   O

M

chapter five

One week had passed since Morton Blacke and Leslie Vitter first dined together on Misty Lane. They had shared much since that splendid bottle of *Silver Oak*, complementing some mouth-watering rock lobsters and spuds.

They truly enjoyed each other's companionship. Nothing physical, just pure friendship dripping with yearning admirations—yearning pleasures. As for Mr. Blacke's masterpiece, he had written a few new notes and filled in, editing and adding more flavor, but the right ending was yet to be found. It *was* a real masterpiece, though, not an imaginery work of art that kept the publisher's book advances coming in, the type of thing struggling writers have been known to do. But he didn't need the money, not like Osano did in *Fool's Die*.

He had gone to town searching for a muse; but instead, he had found someone of which he was growing deeply enamored. He did his best to block the 'voice of past pains' from slithering into a tiny crevice behind his yellow eyes. It needed to stay away. It needed to sleep... and never awaken on this new, brilliant dawning of sweet, shared remorse.

They decided, on one occasion after a few martinis, with Leslie leading the charge, to touch upon their dreary and mournful pasts. Morton didn't like recalling these memories, but he did it for her. He shared, nonetheless, but with an approach comparable to an out-of-body experience. His tongue rolled off the words and regrets that Leslie had wanted to hear and help with, but his inner soul—the one that couldn't wait to taste infinite success like a vampire seeking blood—was somewhere else. It wasn't listening. It was preoccupied with *All Roads Lead To Damascus*. Morton Blacke wasn't trying to put on a charade for Leslie Vitter; on the contrary, he spoke all truths, but it was just who he was.

On this muggy spring night, the rain that frequently pattered Mr. Blacke's mansion windows, the 'Mansion on the Hill,' returns. But bad weather or not, the new friends are going to Redstone, in search of a mid-evening movie.

Their first stop is west of Lago Diablo, on the outskirts of Wickerton. It really isn't too far out of the way on their path to Redstone. Morton and Leslie have an early dinner at The Horseshoe, a well-known barbecue joint with exceptionally good baby back ribs and delightful, fresh-brewed iced tea.

They eat and move along, nothing exciting. Morton pulls his fast car into downtown Redstone; it is movie time. The theater, named after the small town, showcases an early 1900s vertical sign—REDSTONE in protruding metal letters. The overhead to the entrance is dotted with large neon lights of red, green, and yellow. The old-fashioned booth is a one-seater, jutting out from the doors marked entrance and exit. The cinema features three film selections on three screens. Morton and Leslie want to watch something they both think would entertain as well as stimulate their hungry minds; they choose Frank Miller's graphic novel, "300," prepared for the big screen.

Armed with a large Coca-Cola classic and buttered popcorn, the attractive pair find the intimate seating quite empty. This isn't a reflection on the movie itself, but rather the condition of the diminishing downtown area of Redstone. People were moving further away from this rock town, closer to the Wal-Mart just outside the limits, once known for its prosperous quarry now nearly drained. But the founders and faithful Redstone residents remained. And that was enough to keep tourism alive and provide an adequate living for one's family.

The movie is underway...

b l a c k e

"Where to now?" Morton asks, opening his silver BMW's passenger door for Ms. Vitter as she runs to get out of the sprinkling drizzle. She had laughed on the second time Morton had come to her home, driving a different vehicle than the red Ferrari on their first so-called date. And then she had laughed again, when a couple of nights later, he showed up in his Hummer. 'I like the variety, keeps things fresh,' Morton had responded.

He walks around to the driver's side, dropping into the beamer's seat with a newfound hop in his step. Quite possibly, it could be because of the water coming down, wetting his shiny black hair.

"So where is it we're going?" Morton asks again, plopping into his seat. His face resembles a handsome Harrison Ford, with darker hair, but those same soft eyes, full of mystery and intrigue.

"I'd like to see your home... someday," Leslie answers, her face reflecting that head-turning smile that never ceases to amaze him. The word 'someday' is in reference to the fact that she hadn't yet been to the proclaimed, 'Mansion on the

Hill.' In the beginning, she preferred the comfort of her own place. And Morton, she believed, preferred the comfort of being alone in his own castle.

But she is ready to move forward. If, that is, Morton is as well. "I think I can arrange that," he says, starting the engine. The luxury car's motor purrs with the sweet sounds of refined power. He puts it in reverse and backs out of the movie theater's parking space.

"Are you sure?" Leslie asks, wanting things to continue to be so smooth and easy. She didn't want to force anything; she didn't want to be the reason for things becoming uncomfortable.

"I'm positive." Morton always has a tough time keeping the throttle down as he moved the gorgeous car through the inner part of Redstone. He heads for Route 163, *still think it should be called Loop 163 as it takes me home via a loop...*

And on their fourth night together, Morton and Leslie travel to a new destination. Alas, she would get to see the world famous author's headquarters. Where he dwells... Where he writes... Where he sleeps...

Jumping on the freeway, with the windshield wipers clicked low, Morton pushes back the urge to open his favorite toy up, seeing as though there is a slick dampness on the asphalt. He isn't sure what's going to happen after Leslie and him arrive at his mansion; he guesses that she'll want the tour.

The west wing perhaps? Where things appear "normal." Where the world is right and the light is reflected off pleasant colors. He will save the east wing, with the 'evil kitchen' and the hidden money in the octagon playroom, for later. Leslie deserves better. She should be shown the magnificent aspects of the house; the birch table in the dining room and the unique, bold-framed artwork aligning the high walls and the breathtaking foyer ceiling and the shelf after shelf of glass-cased writing awards and accolades. These were the things that would intrigue her, not as if she needed any more cajoling. She didn't need to know about the east wing and its secrets right now.

"I'm surprisingly very excited. Like a young girl," Leslie says, giggling at the last words that leave her mouth. She kicks off her open-toed sandals and puts her bare feet up on the dashboard. She's gotten a peek at some of Morton's peculiar ways, but she knows he won't mind the new resting place for her walking buddies.

"You should be." Morton grins, glancing in his rearview mirror and switching lanes. They zoom South, with the exit for the windy, uphill "Author Lane" nearing, nicknamed by the five towns' newspaper, the *Lago Diablo News*.

"Oh yeah? Why's that?" Leslie asks. She removes her feet from the dash and sits up, leaning forward and cocking her head towards Morton. That dazzling smile still remains.

"Well..." Morton flips on his blinker, even though there aren't any other cars on the road. He switches lanes. "Because *you* are about to get the grand tour, that some people would die for. You are quite the lucky woman, Miss Vitter. You should cherish this moment forever."

"You're such an ass," she says, and they both laugh. "But you're right about one thing... I am a lucky woman."

"You can say that again." Morton tries to keep a straight, stern face, but fails miserably. He can't pretend to be serious around her; she brings out the pure humor within.

"Ass!" Leslie yells jokingly. She reaches over and messes up the writer's thick hair. Morton does nothing to stop her. He only carries with him that confident, friendly smirk and drives on. He exits Author Lane and presses down harder on the gas, climbing. He then lets off the pedal as the first of many sharp turns sinuously greet the driver all the way to the black-iron double gate with a large 'B' intertwined in the metal bars. Half the 'B' is on the left gate, the other half is on the right gate.

After some silence, the BMW rounding the corners with controlled precision, Morton, possibly a little late, says, "You know? My hair was already messed up from the rain."

"In that case," Leslie begins. "I think it looks better now."

"Ass," Morton says. They exchange warm smiles for the millionth time since their first meeting. Morton Blacke presses the tiny remote, clipped to his beamer's visor, and opens the daunting, entry gates.

b l a c k e

After hours of opening doors and walking halls and climbing stairs, interestingly looking at every nook and cranny, Leslie begins to feel the late hours coming. She yawns as Mr. Blacke shows her his west wing office and antique typewriter that produces the acclaimed novels—she simply loves the expensive throne he writes from.

"Getting bored?" Morton asks.

"No. Sorry. Just a little sleepy." Leslie covers her mouth, trying to avoid a second yawn. According to her, tonight's date is going perfectly. She has no complaints. She feels the blossoming romance stirring in spring's sticky air.

Did Morton reflect her growing, emotional attachment? She ponders this question in her mind. She will find out soon enough.

"Shall I take you home then?" Morton's tone is all Leslie needs to hear. She recognizes the want... the same feeling that flows in her veins. She believes he is interested in her staying the night as well. Leslie goes for it.

"I really don't feel like going down to Misty Lane tonight," she says and then waits. She waits for her new friend's response. She waits for her life to change in a new, hopefully promising direction.

The light bulb triggers inside Morton's head. A once dark room now gleams with a fluorescent brilliance. He smiles at Leslie; she staring at his deviating expressions.

"Do you want to stay the night?" Calm and confident.

Finally... Leslie thinks. The magic words.

"That would be simply... splendid," she says, reaching for his hand. Morton takes it without trepidation and guides her back to the center of the mansion. They pass through the west wing hallway and enter back into the 'Great Passageway' before arriving at the spiral staircase's marble landing, nearer to west wing than the east wing, the first step as sparkling dark as the night sky.

With his right hand interlocked with hers, and his left

hand tugging gently on the stair's metal banister for nothing more than mindful assurance, the couple ascends the steps to the second floor. They zag in a straight-up direction, circling the skeleton stairs. Their path... the master bedroom.

They arrive in the unlit landing area—their heads popping up and out of the stairwell like a gopher's.

Why is there no light in here? Leslie thinks, gripping Morton's hand tighter as her vision is most definitely lacking.

I've got to get that light fixed, Morton thinks, feeling Leslie's hand squeeze a little harder. *Some people enjoy the lighting, Morty. Especially when they don't know where they're going.*

With memorized steps, Morton plays guide, turning to his left and heading towards the master bedroom's door. He reaches for black metal—molded for a welcoming hand—thumbing the trigger that allows entry. Morton gently pushes the heavy door open, it swings to his left and reveals an incredibly large room pushed right of the entrance.

With glowing moonlight casting an eerie light, Leslie sees the door's foot-long, vertical handle. It reminds her of one that was located on her parent's back gate, used to enter the backyard hidden inside a tall, wooden fence. Except

Morton's is much more unique, with a customized grip fitting snug with his right hand and rich metal-work that appeared lavish.

The door, itself, is built of six, deep-stained Redwood planks, with flat, black metal strips, very similar to the handle, serving as dividers for the attached wood.

Morton takes a few steps into the master bedroom. Leslie tags along right behind him. She releases hold of his hand; instinct tells her to place both of her hands to her cheeks... in awe. *Wow!* The one-word exclamation shouts in her head and then aloud.

"Wow!" she says, the magnifying word partially distorted by her hands pressing against the sides of her face. Morton moves from her side, not in an attempt to get away, but to allow Leslie to take in the overwhelming room.

She sees...

A bedroom that is somewhere around thirty-by-thirty feet in size, with an open archway leading to what she could only imagine being the master bath and closet. A thick, toffee-colored, six-inch chair rail of exotic carvings and lettering wraps the enormous room. The majority of the four walls, above the rail, are painted a deep red; this reminds Leslie of dried blood, no matter how hard she tries to not be morbid. The less significant, lower part of the walls are painted a darker brown than the trim above it. On the outer wall, opposite of the door leading into the room, two large, casement windows, that latch from the inside, opening outward, jut out from the wall just above the wood railing, leaving a two-foot bench. The ceiling is vaulted, adding to the spectacle. The hardwood floor below is surprisingly very smooth, yet cold and entirely uncovered.

The furniture, however, is very sparse. An antique rocker with a small nightstand—a chess table etched and stained into the wood—sit beside the first window. Other than the master bed, which can hold its own, there is nothing else. No paintings and no pictures... no nothing. The bed that Morton sleeps in is huge, at least a double-king, and features a wraparound frame with delicately-carved wood spires and a black-laced canopy. Hiding inside the frame, underneath the custom-overhead, is a crystal clear mirror.

Leslie stands near the bed, glancing up. "Not conceited at all, huh?" she asks, but she's only joking. Her sweet smile says everything. She truly loves his confidence.

Morton moves closer to her again. He looks underneath the canopy, up at himself. "I prefer vain."

Before Leslie can respond, he wraps his arms around her and pulls. They tumble together into the marshmallow-soft bed. Morton presses against her, his face now inches away from hers. He leans in, his mouth connecting with her soft, full lips. Without any hesitation whatsoever, Leslie welcomes the gentle kiss, returning the favor by allowing the tip of her tongue to sneakily slip through and encourage Morton's passion.

Morton rubs her back with one hand while caressing her long brown hair with the other. Leslie's focus is centered on the romantic kisses. After a few seconds of a "lovers' exchange eternal," with lips locked, they move apart simultaneously for a quick breath.

"Everything okay?" Morton questions without thinking something is wrong. It is a simple, sweet gesture, coming from one who knew the pains of losing someone in the past. He only wants to make absolutely sure Leslie is in complete harmony with him, not wanting to apply any undesired pressure.

"It's perfect," Leslie answers, her face moving closer again. She's ready for round two.

The new lovers kiss long hours past midnight. They lie in Morton's oversized bed on Down pillows, sharing sexual thoughts and witty stories of their previous existence.

They do not make love. Neither Morton nor Leslie push the issue. Neither one of them caring. They are happy just being in one another's arms and spending one night, at least, with loneliness waiting outside on the doormat. Loneliness, a 'he' in Leslie's case, wouldn't be coming in out of the cool, spring breeze on this night. 'He' better go for a nightly stroll and find someone else to bother.

'He' might as well travel down the hill, back to Lago Diablo, and to an empty house on Misty Lane.

T
O
R
O
M
O

<u>chapter six</u>

It had been nine years since the murder of my best friend, Jeffrey Jane. I had put my writing on hold, still raking in the profits made from one of the all-time bestseller's, *Every Dog Has Its Night*. It was a severe break, and few and far between critics said that I was going to be a flash in the pan. They thought that I might be a one-hit wonder. One and done. How wrong they would be...

And not only that... but there weren't too many authors who remained in the limelight, despite not publishing anything over twenty pages in such a lengthy time. They should have known I would return to the crest of the literature mountain.

Instead of writing, I focused on my education, distinguished level after distinguished level.

I really wanted to teach at my alma mater, but they already boasted one of the top notch English professors in the country. Armed with a Master's degree from Johns Hopkins and a Ph.D. from Columbia, I had taken an offer from Harvard University, becoming the youngest professor in the history of the school. It didn't hurt that despite only having one, true novel published to my credit, I was a worldwide writing celebrity. Every newspaper, talk show, and book magazine coveted me, continuing to pry on the details of my second novel, building its hype for those long, nine years.

Following advice from a fellow colleague, I leaked an excerpt, about a month before release, from my new novel to the *Cambridge Chronicle*. They ran with the preview, flashing around a front-page article that boasted, "A First Peak at Blacke's Return." Not only did it cause some early, east coast buzz, but it riled up the other major newspapers across the nation. They were practically banging down my door. The pot was stirred...

With a year of teaching under my belt, I had been secretly putting together my second masterpiece until now. It was finally time for the long-awaited, *A Dozen Blacke Tales*, to be released. The early reviews and hysteria were taking the literary world to another dimension. Some were even speaking Pulitzer Prize, *the* author's award that my fans believed I was snubbed, back in '86.

The only debate that arose against my lengthy fiction novel was that it featured twelve different tales, totaling just over eight-hundred pages. The dazzling part... each of the twelve stories boasted a streaming connection that could only be revealed to the reader by completing the entire work. Most critics believed a book not entirely built upon one storyline—one setting—wasn't eligible for such a prestigious award, but my diehard followers didn't agree.

They spoke up from behind their review desks located in high-rise suites with drop-dead downtown views. They praised, they begged, they called for justice from the *Washington Post*, "If any author is ever one-hundred percent deserving of the Pulitzer, it's Morton Blacke."

I had two other people in my corner as well, which meant more to me than any newspaper hack or critic. One was my fiancé, Sierra Jamison, a beautiful blonde from the west coast with pearl eyes and long legs. She came from a wealthy California family, her father, Tom Jamison, made his money in a rapid succession with early investments on solid tips in the computer business during the eighties. This allowed Sierra, and her mother, Sally, to go shopping on Rodeo, and tanning, and take dance lessons, and spend long hours at San Francisco Beach. She was a destined housewife, but the way her eyes looked at me day after day, with all the love and care in the world, I promised I would take care of her as long as she'd have me.

The other was my beloved friend and colleague, the man whom I sought advice from daily, a highly-sought after speaker, and one of Harvard University's finest in the literature department, Professor Patrick Parkey. He was twenty years my elder, with flowing white locks resting upon a head of hair thicker than plush carpet, but we shared deep talks of wisdom over exquisite lunches every work day. He had been a major factor in my choice of universities to teach; I truly looked forward to hearing him speak every, single time he opened his mouth or approached a microphone. He was just that damn interesting. And we had rapidly grown very close—an unknowing mentor if I may.

Sierra accompanied me to my book-release reading and signing. We wanted to host the event at Johns Hopkins Main Library, the last place Jeffrey Jane had been—reading *Every Dog Has Its Night*. But their building had already been booked by some pop singer signing her new album. We settled nearer Harvard, at my favorite type of venue—a bookstore. It was going to be a chaotic event, nevertheless.

My fiancé sat in the first row, a few feet directly in front of me, as I read excerpts from *A Dozen Blacke Tales*. I took questions and enlightened those curious, yearning minds that were my dearest fans. Then I moved to a designated table, readied with a sharp-tip marker, to let the book signing begin.

The line was endless. It started at the back of the large Barnes and Noble Prudential Center in Cambridge, Massachusetts, where I was seated in the marked-off area, and traveled all the way out the front door and down several blocks of Boylston Street. I didn't think I was ever going to leave that day. But with Sierra at my side, encouraging and sharing in the laughter initiated by comic fanatics, everything seemed perfect.

But it didn't feel perfect...

It felt like the last time. It felt like the Dwight Evans baseball card combined with Every Dog Has Its Night. I could see a full moon smiling at me with the devilish grin that I loved to imitate.

The moon was the same one that lighted my master bedroom located in the 'Mansion on the Hill.' Not literally. But poetically taunting my life with a higher power plucking my chords of fate.

The smile was... Jeffrey Jane's.

b l a c k e

Five thousand sets of eyes followed the speaker's every move.

Every raise of his fist, every removal of his uniquely-detailed bifocals, every scratch of his white-haired scalp, every step to one side or the other, and every sip of water from an idiosyncratic, jeweled glass resting on a black stool, Professor Parkey captured another mesmerized crowd's undivided attention. At two-hundred dollars a pop for tickets, a small percentage going to a charitable cause, no one expected anything less.

While I was signing more copies of *A Dozen Blacke Tales*, my fellow colleague and good friend lectured as the sun was going down, leaving an azure sky to its own dark fate.

"So this leads us into another realm of opening doors, shutting faster than we can squeeze through them. This leaves a deep scar down the center of our curious minds, dug just enough to draw crimson, but nowhere near the vital core. Our eyes sting with liquid drops of spiteful determination. We kick at the closed doors. One after another, swift blows fueled by, in most cases... anger. But in some special circumstances... measured redemption. We kick so furiously that literally, we've got our foot *in* the door." Professor Parkey took another gulp of his water as the audience first laughed, then applauded. The speaker continued.

"We scream, 'Please! Please! Just give me a chance! I

know I can do it!' But they just shake their robot heads and ask over and over and over... 'Why you?' And then, my dear, dear listeners, we haven't thy answer. Old English if I may, just a taste. One word. We haven't *thy* answer. And then you ask yourself... 'Why?' And then the vicious cycle repeats itself until your tired of kicking and your big toe is swollen lavender and possibly broken. And this all happens because... because instead of learning *why*, you just settle for your own preconceived notions at how good you are and how there can't be others similar or better and how easily it becomes to take this ruthless, charred world for granted."

The professor took a deep breath, collecting his next thoughts. The audience saw the opportunity to applaud again, with echoed claps of enthusiastic hands colliding. Professor Parkey was ready to finish this masterful speech.

"So this leads us into another realm of opening doors, this time shutting even faster than before. We can't even—"

Before another word could exit the professor's mouth, his right hand was at his throat, his left hand was holding his chest. He dropped to one knee and then another. Most of the audience didn't know if this was part of the lecture or something else. They asked themselves 'why' instead of acting with any instinct. A few people had begun to rush the stage.

Professor Parkey fell face-first into the hardwood. He kicked several times, gasping for air, before a frightening still overcame his motionless body.

The first person to hop onto the stage yelled, "Somebody call an ambulance!"

People rose from their seats, all wanting to help, but none knowing the best way as the aisles were already flooded with panicky spectators. The backstage security had come front and center, two of them tried to perform CPR on the limp mass of flesh.

It was no use. Professor Parkey wasn't breathing. The paramedics were too late. His death was later diagnosed as a severe heart attack. For everyone in attendance and everyone else around the world, it was just a tragic lose. Nothing anybody could do. Professor Parkey would be deeply mourned.

But for me... it was more. It wasn't just an early death for a man in his late forties. It was something that had to do with me—Morton Blacke.

I received that dreadful phone call a couple of hours before midnight. I had already been getting in the spirit, or lack there of, with a poured glass of Woodford—something I typically splashed over a little ice and water if I wasn't feeling like wine—about thirty minutes prior to the expected ringing. I wasn't saying that I could predict the future. If I could, things would have been much different. I wasn't implying that I possessed any extra foresight or feelings than the average person did. No way.

But with a record-breaking opening day, the book sales skyrocketing right through the roof, I didn't expect anything less. Not with the novel, *A Dozen Blacke Tales*. Not with the death of a dear friend, Professor Parkey. I know, you are already tying it in with my past. This magical correlation between my success and people (and animals) close to me dying. It was still absurd. The thought... the notion... the accusation. I don't deserve to be treated like a monster because of what? Because of another wicked coincidence? Because of something beyond my control or power?

I wrote books. It was that simple. I yearned for the riches and wealth of our short life—one time around in my opinion. What was so wrong with that? What was so wrong with me?

I answered the phone with butterflies—*these* fluttering around with spiked wings—in my stomach. I had no idea what the call was going to be about. I had no idea it involved my colleague, someone I truly admired and imitated, Professor Patrick Parkey. I did, at least I believe I did, feel something was wrong.

And then the woman's voice, Anne something, on the other side clarified my evil suspicions. She was also a Harvard colleague, an assistant prof in the law department. She told me the usual. How sorry she was. How there was nothing anybody could do. How tragic a loss this was. Etcetera... etcetera... etcetera...

I hung the phone up. I took another sip of my chilled whiskey. A part of me was shredded into bloody bits of sadness and sorrow. A part of me hated this awful world for its conniving ability to toss one a bone of great fortune, but after gnawing on that bone with an unmatched feeling of accomplishment, and then burying it for later, one would only find that the much-anticipated second helping was sprinkled with a new poison... a new disease that pissed on your happy parade. This was life in general. Not necessarily my life. You are the one that read more into these events than you should. You are the one that made me, Morton Blacke, feel different—an outcast. My peculiar ways are simply that... *my* peculiar ways.

And then there was the part of me that remained "unscarred."

Trust me, I'm a famous author. I understand that "unscarred" isn't a Dictionary word per say, but it is the best adjective for the situation. So just roll with it.

That unscarred shell loved the success, craved the masses, and thrived on the praise, one review after another, regardless of what happened around me. Death did not faze me. I don't believe I ignored it as much as I still really didn't believe my actions... my writings... had anything to do with anything in the world except to make my fans and readers have something to look forward to and make their simple lives a modicum better.

They deserved it. People deserved to feel enlightened... to feel they had just read something noteworthy. Fans wanted to share with other readers the dazzling words that I had sprinkled across cream paper.

My successes would not end now. If it had been my fiancé, Sierra Jamison, who had died, I don't know what I would have done. The demons inside me said, 'You would have kept on writing... you would have kept on selling novels."

But I didn't want to believe that—

There wasn't any correlation between... between... *what were we comparing again?*

Nothing more.

Nothing less.

T

R

O

N

O

M

chapter seven

Aching, cramping, stinging fingers pounce like a black jungle panther on passing prey, striking the keys with precision guided by none other than a fresh motivation—a new muse.

An ink-filled stack of pages rests beside the antique typewriter. Adjacent to the latest-typed manuscript lies a sea blue fountain pen—the name MORTON BLACKE printed along the grip. Just beyond the paper is a solid black coffee mug, filled with what works best; its only blemish, a speck of white showing on the outer part of the rim where it had previously chipped.

Mr. Blacke didn't know how that happened. One day it was flawless. The next—damaged. It didn't matter anyway, the words were flowing again. From his mind, passing the heart for a quick scan, usually that organ didn't do very much monitoring, down his right and left arms, to the tips of his fingers, and then onto the "special" cream paper—no smudge, no smear. The black ink was doing its best to keep up with his speedy mind, storytelling at its pinnacle.

Leslie Vitter, who had been rotating stays between her cozy cottage on Misty Lane and the overwhelming 'Mansion on the Hill' with Morton Blacke for over a month now, had just left to work.

The couple had moved along nicely, especially in the last two weeks. Both of them, even though Morton rarely reflected on his melancholic past and the saddening reflections sparkling in life's translucent fountain, had put aside any uncomfortable new feelings and welcomed a fresh chance at love with open arms. This was more beneficial for Leslie, not only as a woman, but also as someone who seemed to be occasionally overwhelmed by flooding memories full of sorrow and regret. Morton, in addition, had even stopped driving his wife's red Ferrari, thinking this would help to show Leslie Vitter of his willingness to move forward and assure her of how fond he was of her.

Morton Blacke is eager to write some more, but he's already been missing Leslie since she drove off in her Aviator, heading to the Montaville Veterinary Clinic. She served as the lead Vet Tech, assisting with the most delicate animal injuries that ranged from fine-tuning expensive quarter horses to the recovery of full-bred canines. Ms. Vitter mastered each animal with not only a studied accuracy, but also a superb experience that could only derive from handling critical cases straight out of Youngstown State University. She hadn't wasted any time, immediately entering the veterinary business and rising faster than most.

A few months back, Leslie had shared with Morton that she had been personally selected by Trot Lang, a once local horse trainer, who moved to Kentucky to be closer to the big race, to work on a prestigious thoroughbred named *Cider Apple*. The horse had suffered one foot injury after another, each previous specialist temporarily solving the problem. But once the races began, *Cider Apple* either came out hobbled or ended with a limp.

"Well... what happened?" Morton had asked.

"Nuthin', hun. I told Trot there wasn't anything that could be done. He took my word. And *Cider Apple* was retired, put out to stud."

In the octagon-office of Morton Blacke's west wing, the sun is out, and it is almost noon. The light is partially blocked by wood shades. The brilliant writer's right-hand index finger presses a 'y,' and then within a flash, almost invisible to the naked eye, his right-hand ring finger strikes an 'o,' and then before the right-hand index finger can even get an inch above the keys, it connects with a 'u.'

The crisp pages continue to be filled like icing on a

cake. The only music in the room is the harmonious rapping of the typewriter, beating to the bones inside his magical ten digits. It plays the sweet sound of new thoughts, a clearer vision with the proper diatribe of rich characters and their newfound paths unraveled—a perfect amalgamate.

Mr. Blacke closes his eyes. But his fingers don't stop. He plays out a brief picture, stamped against the inner blacks of his eyelids. The visualizations help smoothen, clarify, the neo-scenes taking shape in *All Roads Lead to Damascus*. Thanks to Leslie. Thanks to his muse. *I'm going to finish this stubborn book at last. And then all those impatient bastards and hacks waiting to get their spiny fingers on a copy for free, for review, will have—*

Mr. Blacke's phone is ringing. It rings with a sharp buzzing, quick and to the point. The startling noise fills every room in the mansion. He jumps in his seat, frowning at himself for forgetting to pull the lever. Morton Blacke rises from his throne. If the antique producer-of-words could speak, it would say, 'thank you for giving me a break... thank you for not banging on me anymore.'

Mr. Blacke prepares to leave the office, neatly stacking all the typed pages. He sets the signature fountain pen atop the paper, diagonally across the top page. The buzzer chimes again. He shakes his head, proceeding towards the center of his castle. He opens one door, leading into the west wing hallway, and closes it behind him. He sees a picture of Hunter. S. Thompson and himself both holding shot-guns—the photo taken after an adventurous day of hunting doves. The phone buzzes again, forcing him to continue on and leave the memories behind. He walks the rest of the hall without stopping for any sight-seeing. He opens the next door, leading into the 'Great Passageway,' and then closes it as well.

Despite the unimaginable size of Morton Blacke's mansion, the present household only has one phone. You might think this seems peculiar, but that's the way Mr. Blacke wanted it, after Sierra's death, and that's the way it is.

He ascends the spiral staircase with a hop in his step, eager to cease the disturbing buzz that not only annoys him, but also the fabled ghosts that walk the walls every night in the mansion. Mr. Blacke shoots up through the second-floor opening like a Jack-in-the-box. Another sound fills the silent mansion, long and man-made, a forced disruption. Mr. Blacke lets out a relaxing sigh.

"Goddamn barking spiders," he says aloud as he arrives on the second-floor landing. "Spend your whole life trying to get rid of all of 'em, but when you least expect it, they sound off, letting you know they're still around."

He takes a few steps towards the east wing guest bedroom and the closed room, symmetric in size to his upstairs master bedroom, closet, and bath, but not a mirror image in reference to design and layout. He pauses, lifting his right leg a little off the hardwood. He pushes out another amusing sound; this one with a lower decibel level and not quite as lengthy.

"Gotta' straggler."

He reaches for the traditional doorknob—mahogany in color—which leads to a miniature hallway, featuring a few self-portraits of his late wife and late son. The different art works are done by a variety of painters, each using their own, distinguished styles, ranging from the brush types to the actual background the painting would take form. One painting features a colored-pencil sketch, another one features delicate brush strokes on canvas, another one features bright watercolors, and on and on.

As the door, a slightly lighter black-red than the knob, begins to swing open towards the short hall, Morton Blacke hears a clamoring echo downstairs. *You've got to be shitting me?* He recognizes the sound—metal meeting wood. *I just want to pull the fucking lever already.* He laughs to himself, scratching his forehead. The phone's ringing has at least stopped chiming.

The bronze knocker strikes the mansion's medieval oak double-doors for a second time. Mr. Blacke hates this. *Knock once... if nobody answers... then it wasn't meant to be. Pack up and move along buddy.* He holds his hands, palms up, chest high and out in front of him. He glances at one hand and then the next. Mr. Blacke pretends to be a human scale, weighing his options in each hand, the balance teetering for one side and then for the other.

"Son of a bitch," he decides. He turns, closing the dark door, located in east wing of the upstairs, behind him. His bare feet slide across the cold, wooden floor, before meeting with the even cooler marble stairs. He arrives at the bottom, back in the massive foyer and on the first floor of the mansion. He heads down the 'Great Passageway' towards the menacing front doors. Beneath his breath, he whispers, "All I need know is for that damned phone to ring again."

And then, upon request, the phone calls again and the buzzer returns. Someone else is now calling his home. It fills the foyer for approximately two seconds, trumpeting along with Morton Blacke's stroll to the front of his castle like a following band. He comes to a halt a foot short of the doors, blowing air into his cheeks, appearing similar to a blowfish. He rolls his eyes back into his head. The buzzing occurs again. *Stop ringing already!*

He swings open the large oak door on his right. You might think he was greeting a shopper-frenzied rush, the morning sales just open for business. He smiles his lovable grin, flashing his convincing teeth. He speaks to the stranger.

"May I help you?"

b l a c k e

Several things dance inside Morton Blacke's mind all at once, butterflies floating in a summer's breeze.

He keeps returning to the lever. He can see the second guest room in the upstairs east wing. He can see the early 1900s wooden wall telephone, hanging just inside the bedroom door. Slightly to the phone's left, on the same line of sight, a two-foot long, black steel handle protrudes from the wall. *The lever.*

If one pulled the lever from its current 'on' position, jutting at a forty-five towards the high ceiling, down to its 'off' position, where Mr. Blacke kept it ninety-nine-point-nine percent of the time, this would completely cut off all outside oral communication. Mail would still be delivered outside the 'B' engraved metal gates, but definitely no more voices on the other side.

Mr. Blacke didn't carry a cell phone. A hermit didn't need one. And his only house phone, the wall-hanger in the second guest bedroom, could be shut off from the irritating outside world with a pull of the black lever. Why was the lever set in the 'on' position then, one might ask?

It's quite simple. Morton had raised the bar for Leslie to return a work call; her cell phone not getting good service in Morton's residence. It was as if the 'Mansion on the Hill,' possibly fueled by the ghosts in the walls, didn't want contact with the outside world either. Nothing coming in. Nothing going out. Morton Blacke and his eerie surroundings were on the same page—no pun intended.

And so, Mr. Blacke forgot to lower the black lever. Hence the ringing... hence the head-shaking from his forgetfulness this morning.

Now, staring at this long-haired young man on his white-rock front steps, Mr. Blacke realized he forgot something else. He didn't remember to click the iron gates closed—the greeting gates to his castle's courtyard—when Leslie left for the veterinary clinic. That's how the hippie fellow got this far, standing before him with his sweaty hand leaving an oily stain on his matching iron stair-railing, with interlaced metal spires twisting above the stairs parallel rail, constructed more for its dazzling and daunting appearance rather than for a stair-climber's support. It could be very dangerous; the spear-tipped crests of the spires would easily slide through one's palm like butter if a person wasn't cautious.

Mr. Blacke had put this railing in after his son's death; it served as a personal shrine, or memoir, for him. It was his own tribute that he could secretly use for remembering, even if he elected to forget. It also seemed to scream out, 'outsiders not welcome.'

Get your hand off my railing creep, Morton Blacke thinks, waiting for the man in his early twenties to state his reasoning for being there.

"Dude, you got a fuckin' kickass place, man..." The youthful hippie accents the 'man,' adding a sheepish twist. He swipes a sticky nest of brown hair away from his forehead. The humidity is high, but this fellow, with a couple of dark wet areas on his Iron Maiden tee, had apparently been doing some sort of physical activity prior to his arrival.

"Yep, it's not too shabby," Mr. Blacke doesn't quite know how to respond, so he plays the part. "Got a kickass pond in the back, too."

"Fuckin' sweet..." The hippie stretches his last word again, as far as it could go. He nods his head, banging his fists together. Mr. Blacke wonders if the visitor is ever going to answer his initial question. Or if he is ever going to address why the hell he is standing on the beautiful white-rock steps.

Mr. Blacke asks again, a humorous sarcasm in his tone, "So do you need anything? Or are you here to just take in the view?"

"Ahh, shit, man. I'm sorry, bro." The hippie uses his thumb to point behind him, over his shoulder. "Back there, a few miles or so, my 'Vette broke down. It's old, man, but it's still a beaut. I mean, smoke comin' out the hood, and just... uhh... fuckin' wasted, man."

Mr. Blacke laughs at the young man's misfortune as the phone finally ceases to ring inside the mansion. The hippie smiles and adds, "Can you give me a lift, man? Or do you have a phone I could use?"

"I can't give you a ride, bro. I'm trying to work." Mr. Blacke continues to play the role of fellow-surfer-dude, finding it quite easy due to the variety of characters he'd written about in his past bestseller's. "I can't let you use the phone, either. As a matter of fact, I'm trying to get that damn lever pulled."

The hippie appears lost. This makes Mr. Blacke smile that unforgettable smile that literary gurus wanted to take pictures of. The younger man takes a step back. A thought pops into Mr. Blacke's head. He begins with a poll-like question for his own curiosity.

"Do you know who I am... dude?" He almost left the hang-ten ending off, but managed to get it in a little late.

"Nah, man. Just some cool-looking cat with some sweet digs and fuckin' kickass crib. I just need some help, bro. I been walkin' and it's fuckin' hot."

"Wait right here. Give me around five minutes or so."

Mr. Blacke doesn't wait for a response. He closes the front door to the mansion, leaving the hippie standing in the sunlight. Morton Blacke walks back down the 'Great Passageway' towards the dining room's white doors. He turns right before arriving, opening the east wing's hallway and heading towards the multi-car garage. He enters the car room, not needing to flick on any lights due to the glowing beams of yellow spraying through the garage doors horizontal windows.

He finds Sierra's car keys lying in a silver tray where he last left them. He removes all the keys from the chain, all except the one to start the motor. He also pulls off a diamond 'S,' dangling and sparkling beneath the streaming light. The only thing left on the bare sterling silver key chain is the starter key and the car's remote slash alarm. He sets the extras back in the tray, and then proceeds to the red Ferrari. He opens the driver-side door, beginning to clean out any pictures and stashed junk. Once the removal process is complete, Morton Blacke clicks the garage-door opener attached to the car's visor, the same remote that opens the front 'B' gates, and starts the engine.

He backs the red Ferrari out of the garage and wheels it around to the front of his mansion. He drives on the destined path, a circular driveway that surrounds a medieval wishing well that could actually be used for drawing water. The block-shaped stones were a flint gray, purposely stacked with a lack of consistency to add to its ancient mood-setting.

He parks the red rocket in front of hippie; the young man backing out of the driveway area and into some well-groomed green grass. Mr. Blacke kills the motor and gets out of the car. One thing he doesn't forget on this forgetful day is to take the gate and garage clicker off the visor and put it in his pants' front left pocket.

The long brown-haired chap doesn't quite know what to expect. He stares at the beautiful ride, unsure of anything that's going on around him. He runs a slimy finger through his hair, his yellow teeth sticking out of his gums as he squints beneath the glaring sun. Mr. Blacke tosses the

Ferrari's keys at the hippie. The visitor reacts quickly, momentarily fumbling them before making a nice grab. His eyes widen as he holds the car keys in front of them.

"It's yours," Mr. Blacke says. "I don't want it anymore."

"No fuckin' way!" the hippie shouts.

"Yes way. Now get the hell out of here. And get a hair cut." Mr. Blacke begins to walk back into the mansion.

"You're the shit, man! This is totally awesome. How can I ever thank you?"

"Tell *them* that Morton Blacke gave it to you. And tell *them* to stop fucking calling me."

For the second time, Mr. Blacke doesn't wait for a response. He disappears back into the mansion, feeling a hidden burden, pushed back with the rest of his unpleasant memories, lifted. He lets out a deep breath, leaning back against the inside of the front double-doors. *Some peace and quiet at last...*

The phone begins to ring again.

b l a c k e

Standing before the wall-hanger, Morton Blacke's curiosity becomes him. He decides to lift the heavy black phone—like cast iron—off its golden hook and place it near his right ear. He greets with a spontaneous *hello there.*

Mr. Blacke immediately recognizes the woman's voice on the other side.

"I can't believe you answered?" Leslie Vitter expresses, sounding completely caught off guard.

"I had a good feeling," Morton responds. "What's up beautiful?"

"I just wanted to verify that you were coming over for dinner tonight? When I left earlier, we were still somewhat undecided... I think. Umm... either way, not a big deal. But I'd love to see you."

"That works for me," Morton says, putting his left hand in his pocket to feel what's there. His fingers rub against a small piece of hard plastic. He recognizes the object as the remote for the front gates—the one he confiscated from the red Ferrari before the Iron Maiden-loving hippie won the lottery. Morton adds, "I've had an eventful day so far anyways... too many interruptions to get any real work done."

"Oops..." Leslie says. "I'm sure my phone call didn't help. I'm guessing you forgot to... to... what's the amusing saying you use?"

"I forgot to pull that damn lever again."

She laughs on the other side. He smiles in the guest bedroom. "Well... I'm sorry," Leslie says. "Hope things settle down a bit for ya'. I'll be home around five. So come by when you're ready."

"That sounds wonderful," Morton says. "I should be there not an hour later."

"Perfect."

"See you soon."

"Okay, Morty. Bye."

"Bye Leslie."

b l a c k e

With the lever pulled, with some peace and quiet at last, with everything seemingly back to the norm, Mr. Blacke rocks in his master bedroom chair.

He isn't writing. Nor has he written anything since talking to Ms. Vitter. His fingers... his eyes... his mind... need a break. So there he rocks, already dressed for a trip to Misty Lane.

Morton Blacke isn't an avid golfer. He hasn't played in a few years. But yet, he has no problem sporting a flashy blue, with black streaks near the shoulders, silk Greg

Norman collared shirt. The traditional golf shirt feels cool on his skin, venting like an opening in an attic. He wears a pair of Dolce & Gabbana black wool dress pants—his belt and his shoes, both polished to a shiny licorice, are also on the expensive side. It's safe to say, Mr. Blacke's taste in clothing is up to par.

He continues to rock, slowing the pace. He checks his left pocket one more time, assuring himself that he remembered to switch the remote from his beige slacks earlier to the pair of pants he's currently wearing.

The remote, which opened the front gates, standing tall and intimidating, with a magnificent 'B' stretching across one to the next; Mr. Blacke has decided would be best in Leslie's Aviator.

He leaves the rocker. He walks through the archway leading to the master bath. He opens a custom-designed wood cabinet right of the sink, reaching for a bottle of an unmarked men's cologne. The bottle didn't showcase any brand, just a hazy glass container with a smell-good potion in the inside. Mr. Blacke dabs a little on his wrists and neck, and then he leaves the master bedroom through the black-metal-lined door.

He descends the spiral staircase, skipping the last step with a small jump. He lands on the thick, rolled carpet, that divides the foyer down the middle, traveling all the way from the front double doors to the dining area's white doors. He feels great. He feels like a man with a questionable past, whether it was entirely his doing or not, that has been granted a new beginning—a free pass.

He moves east, transcending that hallway for the millionth time and opening the door to the three-car garage. With keys already in the ignition, Mr. Blacke fires up the silver BMW and clicks the remote on the visor. He waits for the runway to clear. And then he's off, zooming down the hill to indulge in another pleasant evening with a woman he's beginning to feel helplessly enamored around.

This is exactly what Morton Blacke was shying away from. This is exactly what Morton Blacke was trying to avoid. This is the hermit inside him—the monster inside him—not wanting any more pain, but still yearning for the mass stardom and trying to set the world-prestigious bar ever higher.

As a vicious cycle always does, not the one that repeats the result necessarily, not that effect, but the one that believes it can alter the cause, therefore putting an end to the expected effect and creating a more encouraging, more positive result... it repeats itself.

Morton Blacke's thoughts are diverted as he smiles out

his window, passing a man running without a shirt on, who should clearly be wearing one.

T
R
O
N
O
M
B

<u>chapter eight</u>

"Billy Blacke, did you forget to turn your radio off upstairs again?" Sierra Blacke asked, with sincerity and patience in her tone. A sweet sound that I felt my own mother lacked when I was a child. *Her* words were spoken through a voice that always seemed to carry a nagging or irritating presence. "Today's a big day for your dad, we've got to get moving."

William Blacke, named after my grandfather, a name in which my new agent, David Gregory, thought to be my own twist at trying to get as close to the great William Blake as I could without robbing the grave, stood before his mother with a disgruntled smirk on his face. A look that he could have only learned, and copied with masterful alikeness, from his father.

The boy, just older than three years of age, turned back around in the mansion-he'd-been-born-in's foyer and darted back up the stairs. Mrs. Blacke shook her head, thinking her son's dark hair, which he also got from his father, was a little shaggy and needed a cut. She could hear the swoosh-swoosh of his kid's windpants, which he and his father called "Ninja Pants" because they were all-black and loose-fitting. The boy also wore a custom small t-shirt, which was a mixture of charcoal gray and stop-sign red, with the words *The Surrounding Sounds* printed on the front. It was an early promo handout from Morton's publicist. Sierra calmly waited for her son.

When Billy returned, he and his mother headed through the east wing of the house to jump in her fully-loaded green Tahoe. There wasn't much light in the garage as the sun had only begun to peak over the tallest hill's pine trees. Sierra Blacke put Billy in his child seat, twice making sure everything was fastened properly.

They were leaving the Lago Diablo area to catch a plane. They were going on a "field trip" as Billy liked call them. This morning of travel was leading them to New York, where they would join me, Mr. Blacke, at a special celebration and book signing for *The Surrounding Sounds*.

The novel, which had released a month before, had shattered my previous high marks of *A Dozen Blacke Tales* in 1995, and my debut book, *Every Dog Has Its Night* in 1986. And when my second novel didn't receive the Pulitzer, the free press were in an uproar. They were calling for heads. They couldn't believe that an all-time bestseller wasn't worthy.

But this time around, with a new literary agent and publishing house, Susperia Books, I had finally received the ultimate reward—a Pulitzer Prize of my own. *The Surrounding Sounds* couldn't have been more popular, more in demand, more anything. That was the cause for this significant, historical signing at Times Square. It was, along with myself, on top of the world with no place to go except down. But it had been a month since its release. I shook my head at the trivial silliness that flooded my brain, day in and day out. Those past thoughts of "my fault" washed in with the strong current, but I quickly pushed them back out with the high tide.

The correlation between my masterful works and something tragic didn't seem to exist. I believed that after all this time, these long, long years, it was nothing more than a bizarre coincidence.

Boy was I wrong...

b l a c k e

The private jet, with only five people on board, reached cruising altitude.

It seemed a waste of a flight, but when there was extra money... there wasn't proper planning or disposal, just look at any bureaucratic decision.

There were two pilots, one stewardess, Sierra Blacke, and William Blacke. The mother and son were seated in personal, leather-padded flying chairs, much more roomy and comfortable than a typical airlines coach seat. A light flashed, followed by a *ding-ding* from the intercom speakers.

"Can I go play now?" Billy asked, doing his best to remain buckled and not throw a fit. This wasn't his first flight, and even though he was only three ('three and a half' if you asked him), Billy understood the plane's noises quite well.

"Yes, hun. Let me help you."

"Okay, mommy."

Sierra Blacke unbuckled her own belt first and stood about three-quarters tall. Partially bent over, she moved over to her son and undid the latch keeping him safe. Billy Blacke immediately hopped up, his eyes on the prize across the aisle and a few feet towards the front of the aircraft. His mother motioned for him to 'go ahead.'

"Thanks, mommy." The boy charged down his own imaginary runway, landing softly on a coffee-colored lounge seat. The fancy leather couch was u-shaped, covering all sides of the plane except an aisle-side opening. It had cup holders, built-in remotes for the overhead television-slash-VCR-slash-DVD player, storage bins near the plane's outer wall (mostly stuffed with pre-arranged toys for Billy), and a matching ottoman in the center, fastened beneath the padded flooring to the plane's internal metal with unbreakable rivets.

Across the aisle was mommy's version of fun time. A small wine cooler, showcasing a half-dozen bottles, chilled champagne on ice, and a mini-fridge loaded with rare beers and pocket-rockets of liquor—the kinds you might find in a Louisiana convenient store.

While Billy turned on the cartoon-version of a Tolkien classic, *The Hobbit*, Sierra treated herself, asking the stewardess for a glass of the *Dom Perignon*. Sierra Blacke accepted the drink from the busty blonde, saying 'thank you' while tossing her bleach blonde hair out of her face.

She chewed on her nails, trying hard not to bite around the cuticles. The alcohol would help this bad habit—one that increased dramatically when flying was involved. She leaned back in her leather flying chair, watching her son easily self-entertain just as his father could.

She drank half the flute, not wasting any time with sissy sipping. This happened before the stewardess could even make it to the back of the plane.

"Another glass?" she asked Sierra Blacke.

"Sure." Billy's mother emptied glass number one, handing it over to the stewardess. 'She's must have had a boob job,' Sierra thought. 'I bet she's a little sad that *Mr. Blacke* isn't on this flight.'

The stewardess set up another round of champagne. Sierra took the glass, politely saying thank you and offering the attendant a seat. The bubbly girl (no pun directed at Mrs. Blacke's choice of alcohol) didn't see any harm in taking a break and chatting for awhile; after all, Sierra Blacke *was* in charge.

While the pair of blondes gossiped—the stewardess, not someone Sierra would want to talk with often, sharing personal secrets and advice, wasn't a bad change of pace—Billy slept mid-flight.

The boy went out somewhere along the part of Tolkien's masterpiece where Bilbo finds *Sting*, the perfect weapon for a hobbit. The hairy-footed person from the Shire now had a ring that made him vanish, and a blade that glowed when goblins were near.

A battle of five armies...

A few hours later, the plane safely landed at the John F. Kennedy International Airport, where a driver was waiting, holding a sign with the name 'Blacke' printed on it, ready to whisk the travelers to Times Square.

b l a c k e

The signing went far beyond what an average novelist would consider a successful event. The celebration for the new Pulitzer Prize winner, Morton Blacke, was not describable with mere words.

I signed my last copy of *The Surrounding Sounds*; the man standing before me in his mid-thirties didn't look completely satisfied. I knew he yearned for me to say something more than 'thank you' or 'have a great day,' so I granted his wish.

"Mark Twain once said, the difference between the right word and the almost right word is the difference between lightning and the lightning bug."

The man, with thin brown hair and a revealed front to his scalp, smiled. "Brilliant," he said, appearing to be reciting the quote over and over again inside his head.

He'll never get it right, I thought. *He'll tell his wife. He'll tell his friends. But it will never be as Mark Twain intended, something will be messed up.*

"That's a wrap," I said, getting a hug from Sierra and William.

Billy said, "No more books, daddy?"

"None."

My son smiled and raised his hand. "High-five?"

I nodded and smacked his hand with mine. A few fans and reporters joined in our laughter. A few camera bulbs flashed, getting one last photo of my son and me.

I stood from my padded-black folding chair and shook hands with David Gregory. Despite a few marks and rough spots on his face, Gregory was a handsome man, always sporting a five-o'clock shadow. He was a couple of inches shorter than I, but jogged every morning to remain fit and in good health. His agent's eyes, always searching for the next dollar, were hidden from view.

He offered my family a ride back to the hotel, but I informed him that it was already taken care of. Embracing Sierra, I felt relieved that all the boxes of books, pre-ordered for this event, had been sold and signed. Not one, single copy left.

After saying our farewells, we headed to our suite at the Hilton Times Square, only a few blocks away.

b l a c k e

I never blamed Sierra for the following...

Shit happens.

I was just sorry it happened to William Blacke. He didn't deserve something so tragic, something so devastating, something the demons shouted at me that it was my fault... for my Pulitzer Prize.

b l a c k e

I was sleeping in the Hilton's suite, resting from my adventurous and successful day.

Sierra had taken Billy down to the hotel's exotic pool, featuring lagoon-like surroundings and a man-made, golden waterfall. The gold coloring came from tiny, but bright, lights that were fixed in the decorative stone and flashed on and off. Once in the water, one could dip their head under the rocks and swim beneath the perfectly-placed marble stones.

Billy had jumped in with a cannonball splash, wearing a new pair of orange and black swimming trunks.

Meanwhile, Sierra, tanned poolside with a Cosmo in hand. Not the magazine, but the refreshing drink.

As Billy swam, Sierra began to relax beneath a setting sun's warmth. The breeze was cool on her face, and the nightly air couldn't have tasted sweeter.

Billy yelled, "Hey mom, watch this!"

He jumped from the fake waterfall's top rocks, clearing a couple of lower shelves and landing in the water. He surfaced, eyes large, and laughed. Sierra applauded him, but relayed.

"Please don't do that again, Billy. You might not make it next time, and then I'll have to jump in and save you." She sat up in her pool chair, taking another sip of her drink. Jokingly, she added. "And you don't want mommy to dive in and ruin her brand new Versace dress, do you?"

William Blacke didn't respond. He only kept on swimming around the grand pool, making laps. I never understood why there wasn't anyone else swimming at the pool, or even relaxing poolside as his wife was. But, of course, this was after another one of his novels was having infinite success and selling like bottled water in the middle of the Sahara.

Somehow...

Someway...

It doesn't matter now. The past is the past.

Sierra Blacke dozed off. Maybe it was the alcohol she had consumed throughout the plane ride up to this point, but I never believed it. Others blamed her, but I didn't. Others cursed her, but I only shrugged my shoulders to the point where Sierra wished that I would have placed the blame in her hands, where she felt it was deserved.

She believed that it would have helped her get over this tragedy, if only I would have agreed with the masses. Everyone... I mean everyone... blamed her, including herself. So why couldn't I blame her?

Because...

Deep down, in the blackest part of my suffering heart, I knew different.

And while she was sleeping poolside in her lounger, Billy Blacke decided to do some exploring beneath the fake waterfall's marble stone.

b l a c k e

The coroner said that William must have bumped his head, quite vigorously, on the bottom of the rocks. He guessed that it might have happened while the boy was on his way out from underneath the beautifying effect, rising to the surface prematurely, but he didn't know for sure.

What he did know for sure is that William Blacke, just older than three years of age, drowned in that pool.

My only son. My only child.

Gone forever.

But...

The Surrounding Sounds became my personal, best-selling book of all-time.

And...

It won Morton Blacke his Pulitzer Prize.

T   L O N

R   O

M O B

R O B

chapter nine

"Where are we going?" Leslie Vitter asks. She reclines the BMW's black leather seat to a sharper angle—her hair, labeled brown but nearer a golden shade beneath dazzling bright rays created by the large, shining sun. She shifts in her seat, kicking up her bare feet and resting them on the dash, which bears oily marks from past encounters with her walking buddies.

Morton only smiles and shakes his head. He answers, "To a magical place that's yet to be tainted by society and trampled by uncaring tourists."

"Oh really?"

"Damn straight."

Leslie didn't like his teasing—his surprises. But she would play along only because she knew the end result would be something magnificent. She hadn't known Morton for that long, but one thing she has quickly learned, when he says something is worthwhile... it is.

The silver beamer speeds South, away from the five

towns connected via Route 163, past the 'Mansion on the Hill,' past the final few chapters of *All Roads Lead to Damascus*, to a hidden location, deeper in the hills and trees and seeming a world away—far, far away—from the bustling world, moving like busy red ants, all around it.

Morton and Leslie share laughs. And they exchange those sweet looks of pleasant faces that yearn for more time together—more time in a 24-hour day. He is taking her to a place he hadn't been to since his wife died. He believes the time is now right. He doesn't doubt or question his decision, derived from love, if only love shared by best friends.

The road begins to wind here even more so than on Author Lane. The hills rise to small mountains and the trees' tops reach for the bottoms of the few scattered, pillowy clouds. One full white cloud, a pregnant addition to the smaller batch, momentarily shadows the car, but then the yellow fireball returns, as warm as before.

Morton sneaks a look at Leslie's face, glowing from the natural light. He thinks, 'how soft, how smooth, how beautiful, yet the scars, similar to mine, hide beneath the surface.'

"What?" she disrupts the silence. But in no way is the question directed with any harsh tone or mild irritation.

"You," Morton responds, half-grinning while squinting

and smiling.

"Me?"

"Simply you."

"What do you mean?"

"You've given me a life, outside of the world of writing, the dungeon full of educated words and home-spun sentences, again." As Leslie takes in what's been said, Morton repeats himself. This time, leaving out his poetic flavors that add ambiance and brilliance. "You've given me a life again."

Leslie smiles, unsure of how to respond to something she initially believes to be the sweetest thing anyone has ever told her. With more thought, and a few passing days, Leslie is sure she will wholeheartedly agree with her first reaction.

They ride in silence, a few more miles tallied on the odometer. Morton can wait. After all, he's been waiting a good while for nothing—at least, expecting nothing. But then she came. In the Lago Food Mart of all places.

"I still don't know what to say," Leslie disturbs the peaceful humming of the car's motor a second time.

"Don't say anything," Morton says. "Your reaction, your mannerisms, and your smile have already said everything. Leave it be. Saying something now will probably only make you sound silly."

And then he laughs.

Leslie pushes him playfully as the car swerves slightly, halfway into the oncoming lane. Morton pulls the wheel back to his right, returning to his side of the road and laughs some more. It feels wonderful to let out a good chuckle without worrying about anything except the humor in the moment.

Leslie is about to gently hit him in the shoulder when the car suddenly brakes hard—the tires screeching—and veers immediate right. She screams, grabbing Morton's right arm and falling into his seat. Meanwhile, he continues to laugh.

She gathers herself, sitting back up in her seat to see the BMW heading down a smooth, dirt road. Clouds upon clouds of deep brown bellow out from behind the car as Morton doesn't let off the accelerator.

They charge down the back road, lined with tall Pines and in-between Spruces. Leslie understands that this isn't an unfamiliar place to her navigator. This is somewhere he's been before—more than a few times.

"Sometimes... let me put this correctly." Leslie pauses, an imaginary light bulb floats above her head. The light comes on. "You can be two things at the same exact time."

"Like what?" Morton asks, taking the bait.

"Like the sweetest guy in the world and the biggest asshole I know."

"If you weren't joking about the second part I'd take offense."

"Who says I'm joking?" Leslie asks, trying her damnest to keep the edges of her mouth from turning upward.

"I do. Hurry. Look." Morton's commands divert their conversation. He lets off the gas pedal and points straight ahead.

They both stare. Though Morton has witnessed the scenery before, he feels like its the first time. He shares in his friend's jubilation and awe.

The dirt road comes to an opening and a rounded ending. Encircling the newfound space are unknown mossy trees, un-belonging, the leaves as forest green as money and the moss as gloomy gray as flint rock. The trees' branches dangle above them with spiny fingers—one looks like a conjurer's skeleton hand, pointing his index finger stretched out from his robe.

A single, pebbled path of multicolored stones of cream, and blossom, and crimson, and licorice, and magenta, and aqua disappears into the thick copse. Several birds call at once, each harmonious in their own, but cacophonous together.

Guarding the entrance to the path before them are staggered rows of the Buttercup family, flowers ranging from Monk's Hood to Windflowers to Red Columbines. Their dazzling array of colors battle the pebble's own color spectrum, each trying to win over one's eyes with a variating richness that ranges from light to dark.

Leslie, still in her seat, never notices Morton exit the vehicle. He gently closes the driver-side door and walks around the back of the car. His polished black shoes quickly dull as the soft dirt—almost sand—splashes against the sides, but the ground is soft on the feet.

She is startled by the opening of her own door. Morton extends a hand, and Leslie takes it instantly. He caresses her fingers with his own before gingerly tugging upward. She rises from the low car and is overwhelmed by an abundance of rich and tangy sweet smells that fill the calm air. Leslie sees a few darts of sunlight sparkling on the darker dirt, resembling lost and forbidden rings that dazzle when lighted.

She takes a deep whiff, closing her eyes and pausing to hold the precious aroma, and then lets out a deep breath. She holds Morton's hand, opening her eyes and feeling as relaxed as any other time in her life.

"Ready?" Morton asks, beginning to move towards the

pebbled pathway.

"There's more?" Leslie returns the question, already hoping they were about to head further into the beautiful thicket.

"Of course."

They walk hand in hand. Morton leads her to the path, stopping at the entrance to scoop up a handful of rocks. He lets them slide between his fingers like sand down an hourglass, and then listens as they clash against their fellow path-mates.

He looks at some of the taller, purple flowers. "They match your shirt."

Leslie drops her chin. She smiles, loving the violet cashmere blouse that Morton bought her for their one-month anniversary—at least one month of them knowing one another.

"They sure do."

They continue down the path, the edges becoming more overgrown and dense—the light fading—the sounds and smells ubiquitous.

Morton halts, turning to his left. Buried in twisted vines that weave in colors of green felt and yellow straw, is a marble sculpture, shaped and chiseled to resemble a three-foot high podium. It flourishes a third century B.C. Greek and Roman influence in the designs and style. The tangling plants wrap around its base, around a foot in diameter, and spiral all the way to the platform top, which reveals this unbelievable artifact.

Resting atop the stone podium is an ancient tome, the engraved writings are faded beyond deciphering, and the delicate book is so entangled in the vines, it would probably come apart at the seams and crumble if it anyone attempted to remove it.

Leslie asks the same question that has probably entered many minds before, "How has this remained untouched for so long?"

"The watchers of the path," Morton answers with a confident tone.

"Don't be silly," Leslie says. "Seriously, this is unreal. How can it be?"

"Some things aren't meant to be unraveled. Nature has its protectors... its secrets... as we do. For now, we just have to embrace the beauty of the sculpture and leave our curiosity behind. And hope... and hope, others continue to do the same."

Leslie nods, taking one last, hard look at the ancient statue. They move on. A few more steps and the birds halt chirping. There is quiet in the woods. But not for long. The sound of running water, splashing down against another hard surface echoes down the tunnel-like path. The light returns as the sound of tumbling liquid grows louder.

"Almost there," Morton says.

Leslie doesn't answer. She is in her own trance, the only thing keeping her steady, balanced, and moving forward is Morton's grasp on her left hand. She feels as though she has left her world of being a Vet Tech, a resident of Lago Diablo, a woman of the modern world, and entered some new realm where nothing matters, but love and beauty and nature's finest sights, sounds, and smells.

The path appears to be blocked. Leslie looks ahead of Morton, seeing the colorful pebbles fade away. Trampled grass, not as verdant as the rest of the scenery, takes its place. A thick patch of white and black-tipped mushrooms beckon on their right. Up ahead, leafy branches dip down over the path and stretch across their way like 'caution' tape. Morton pushes through them, holding the branches with his free arm so they don't come back and slap either of them in the face. Leslie ducks through his created opening and raises her head, lightly shaking the hair from her brow. She pulls free of Morton's grip, not out of shame or anger, but to place both hands over her mouth. She rubs them down her chin and along the top of her neck. She takes in another overwhelming, and absolutely flawless, picture.

'It just keeps getting better,' she thinks.

Along the back rock wall and in the center of the grove, a five-foot wide waterfall cascades down many layers and shelves of all sorts of colorfully altered rocks. The easiest to recognize are a shiny limestone and a magnetic ironstone. And about halfway up the the cliff's wall is a large deposit of glistening calcite crystals.

The waterfall ends up in a shallow pond, possibly three or four feet deep. Not all of the water spills directly into this small pond; but instead, it feeds into three separate streams, all on different elevations and heading in their own distinct directions, faintly visible after sinuously traveling a few yards into the plush overgrowth.

The first and second stream both head to Morton and Leslie's left, one a little further away from them and beginning a little higher up than the other. That same first trickle of water gently rolls over large gray rocks, creating its own mini-falls before flowing out of sight. The second stream, exiting the waterfall much lower, boils like a witch's caldron in a pot of dark soil before seeping into a tiny crevice in the spongy earth, forming nature's version of a water percolator.

The third stream lies on their right. It is the lowest layer of water leaving the waterfall's downward pour, before splashing into the pond and forming photo-paper white waves. It travels perpendicular to the grove's opening before elbowing and heading to lower shelves on the cliff's right side. Marshy tufts of clumped green grass surround the bend and hide feet not fully webbed. Morton and Leslie watch in amazement as a great blue heron dives into the clear cyan water, everything from the neck up disappears beneath an Olympic diver's subtle splash.

The bird returns to view, a young rainbow trout flaps between it beak. The heron crunches down a few times and then swallows the fish. A lump forms in the upper-half of its neck, slowly moving downward towards the bird's hungry belly. Once swallowed, the heron continues its hunt, stalking around the stream's edge with searching eyes.

"That wasn't part of the original show," Morton says. "It's something I added just for you."

"Aww... that's sweet."

Leslie grabs his hand again, not believing this place truly exists and wondering if everything she's seen here is only a dream. Morton guides her to a smooth, peaches and cream, rock, around two-feet high and a few feet more in length. Along the side of the cold rock are scabs of lichen, emerald and slimy. The great stone rests at the south end of the diamond pond, which mirrors both Morton and Leslie's radiant smiles. They sit on the rock, embracing and heeding nature's congenial surroundings.

Hours pass.

How many?

Neither of them really care. They act as lovers, as friends, as romantics, kissing and hugging and sharing their pasts once again.

b l a c k e

Morton Blacke decides to do something he's never done before in his life.

Not with a counselor, not with a psychiatrist, not with any mentors, not with his friends, not even with his wife, Sierra.

He speaks to Leslie Vitter about his writing pasts.

No...

Not the walls lined with trophies, plaques, accolades, and even, a Pulitzer Prize award. But rather the twisted turn of events during the aftermath. He conveys the reasons behind becoming a hermit. The reasons he didn't want to be a part of anyone's life, friend or foe—the elimination of all acquaintances to solve his own life's greatest conundrum. Why?

Why did it happen?

Was it a coincidence?

Could it be only a coincidence?

He doesn't believe so. Maybe in his mind—in his head—he can convince himself. But now with Leslie, in his heart, he knows better.

So he tells Leslie Vitter the reason he never wanted to meet her. He shares with her his deepest fears revolving around a future finished manuscript and published masterpiece, *All Roads Lead to Damascus*.

And after all his stunning and staggering insights to what happens after the novel becomes the 'Number One' bestseller, Leslie remains there... by his side. She doesn't shift on her rock, she doesn't act as though she's scared one bit. She only holds him tighter and says.

"We will find a way, Morty. Don't you worry about me. We will find a way."

reagan rothe

TALON TOMB

chapter ten

Sierra Blacke was a mess.

When An Anagram Isn't a Margana wasn't.

It hit number one with a bang, topping not only the *New York Times* bestseller list instantly, but it was also an immediate success in the bookstores—Barnes & Noble #1 bestseller, Borders #1 bestseller, and the highest selling book (in the first week) of all-time on Amazon.

If only things at home were as good.

Sierra and I shared few words in an average week after our son's death. The four years seemed to fly by, not due to overzealously fun times, but due to my constant writing and keeping mostly to myself, and her withering away and wisping from one place to the next like a dandelion seed head in the breeze. She drank too much. She began smoking endless packs of cigarettes. Which was amusing because she had never even lit a cancer-stick before Billy's incident. She traveled to town to run the same errands, over and over, whether they needed to be done again or not.

I thought she acted as a crazy person would. Or...

I thought she acted as someone who couldn't deal with something so tragic.

I never suspected anything else...

Though I never blamed her, I never comforted her either. I dealt with my own pains my way, something she couldn't understand; she needed my help in dealing with her own.

Or, at least, she needed some man's help.

She found this with Henry Lucas and his windblown hair and electric charm.

b l a c k e

He was a fellow author, publishing works that ranged from non-fiction historical events, covering local places that he had lived and traveled, to a few children's books that touched on a delicate subject—children labeled Autistic.

He backed up his legitimate work and research with a Master's Degree in Behavioral Sciences from the University of North Texas. He also carried a minor in English, and Henry Lucas had worked as an editor for the *San Jose Mercury News* straight out of college.

With his experience, expertise, and trusting handsome face, I had sought him out before Sierra and I were engaged. He answered some writing questions for me, and I quizzed him every so often on some of my thoughts, searching for some positive feedback.

Later, he helped with editing *The Surrounding Sounds*, as well as working on my newest release—"another guaranteed masterpiece," quoted the *New York Times*—*When An Anagram Isn't A Margana*.

After I granted him an early read on the unpublished novel, Henry Lucas had said, 'Dammit, Morty, I've read a few novels in my time, including all of your earlier work, but this one is the icing on the freakin' cake. I just don't know how you do it. Over and over. Time and time again. A writer's supposed to eventually decline or at least go up and down a little, but not you. Your work never fails to be more brilliant and more revealing than the last.'

It had nearly made me smile. And since my son's death, I didn't smile much.

I felt connected with this man, very similar to my mentor, Professor Parkey. I hadn't enjoyed someone's company as much as his in a long time, there was no satisfaction or warmth coming from my marriage, and there surely wasn't any happiness during times spent alone, although time did seem to quicken its pace. When I wrote, it was all I thought about. But when my fingers weren't striking keys, few memories surfaced that were festive. Loathsome days and long nights.

Hank and I had become good friends. We went fishing, played occasional golf at the Incarnate Country Club—I was always hitting from the pine needles and getting hammered by Hank, who was a scratch golfer and took pride in being a member, and we had a few beers together at the Yonker's Bar & Grille, which closed a year later.

Henry Lucas enjoyed my company so much, well... he moved to Incarnate.

Little did I know that he wasn't moving just for me.

b l a c k e

The *Lago Diable News* read:

December 7, 2004

Car Crash Takes One Life, Injures Another

On Route 163, heading to Incarnate, Sierra Blacke and friend, Henry Lucas, lost control of his vehicle and crashed into the guardrail above the Hollow River that flows directly from Devil's Lake.

The car wreck took Blacke's life, wife of the famous, bestselling writer, Morton Blacke. Lucas is in stable condition at the Paschal Hill Hospital.

There was mist and fog in the air, and police believe that alcohol wasn't involved.

"There weren't any signs of drinking or drug paraphernalia," Chief-of-Police Dave Graham said. "It just seems they lost control, possibly due to the bad weather."

...story continued on page 7

My favorite part was the "friend" line. Sierra Blacke and *her friend*, Henry Lucas. How about her lover?

Let's try that one.

One could at least get the facts straight. She wasn't driving around with *my* friend—not anymore. She was driving around with her secret lover, something I didn't know until after her death—until Henry paid me an unexpected visit to apologize for something I had already guessed.

Hate me for it, but this was the first time I didn't feel any sympathy or remorse. When I published another masterpiece, and then the scheduled misfortune struck, a part of me always felt something, but I was always able to push it away. I could hide the real pain and guilt, which I didn't feel I deserved and was blamed for only by the demons inside of me.

A part of me always missed, whether I carried the weight or not upon my shoulders: with Smokey, with Jeffery Jane, with Professor Parkey, and with my son, William Blacke. But with my cheating wife, Sierra, I felt nothing.

Congratulations. I might not have been the best husband, especially after such a family tragedy became the number one reason for tearing us apart, but I believed I deserved to be told. I would have given her my blessing if she wanted a divorce and wanted to move forward. It may not have been what I wanted, but I would have honored her wishes. I would have given him my blessing if he would have came to me afterwards and said that he was sleeping with my wife. We might not have been best friends afterwards, but at least we would have been true to who we were and why we were in Incarnate.

If nothing else, I was true to everything but my own work's consequences.

That...

I couldn't control. And plus, I didn't know if it was truly my role to alter or be able to twist that part of my writer's life anyways. As much as I wished I could play that character in one of my novels, even God was beyond my reach.

And then, after all that had transpired, a man that ignored my attempts to get a hold of him, a man that owed me some answers, oh Henry Lucas, decided to knock on my door one month after Sierra's death.

b l a c k e

Where did the 'Evil Kitchen' get its name?

Right here...

I let that bastard come into my home. I even gave him the benefit of the doubt, even though someone who wasn't guilty wouldn't have hidden—wouldn't have disappeared—after getting in a car crash with my wife, who didn't come out of the wreckage alive. I wanted to act as the friend I believed I was, and based on that, give him the opportunity to speak to me one time about his conniving deeds.

I took him into the second kitchen, the one through the doors on the east side of the dining room. I made coffee, no sugar or cream for either of us. Straight black.

If you could drink your coffee like a man... maybe you could act like a man.

Instead of apologizing and simply trying to save face, he offered me everything he had. At least... everything he had in terms of actual money. Cold, guilty, cheating cash. And a big bag full of it for that matter.

"Do you think you can buy yourself some freedom from the guilt that burns inside of you?" I asked Henry Lucas.

"I don't know what I'm trying to do, Morty."

"The days of Morty are long gone, buddy," I said. "You messed that up."

"I know. I'm so sorry. Please, please, take the money." Henry fell from his seat, dropping to his knees. "It is the least I can do. I owe you everything I have."

"No. You owe Sierra everything *you* have. I might not have loved her as much as you did. I might not have treated her like you thought I should. I might not have been able to make her smile after Billy's death. But one thing I did do, I never lied to her. I was never unfaithful to her no matter how many opportunities presented themselves. That, Henry Lucas, is something you'll just have to live with."

"I know..." Henry began to cry. I had seen enough of this tiresome charade. *You can act like a man.* Vito Corleone had said it best. Simple. Perfect.

I told him it was time to leave. He had done enough damage, and I wasn't going to be the one to forgive and forget. I wasn't going to be the one to cleanse his lying soul. He would have to own up to his mistakes and learn to live without his affair—without Sierra.

Hell...

I was doing it just fine.

b l a c k e

Seven weeks after Henry Lucas left the infamous money bag, that has rested beneath a trapdoor in the octagon playroom, that has never been opened or spent, I wrote about his dire outcome in my own words—in its own chapter within *All Roads Lead to Damascus.*

Another tear rolls down his cheek. He rubs at it with his left hand. He turns his head to its side, tilting as though it was the world and the last drop of a salty stream is evaporating beneath the weighted, golden blaze.

"Why her?" he says aloud in a whisper, looking down at the emptied bottle of Da Vinci Chianti laying beside him. The words practically chocked their way out between his reddened lips, rasp and scarred. He pinches the crest of his nose with his index finger on one side and his thumb on the other.

"Why did it have to be her?" he speaks

into the palm of his hand.

He pulls his weary body off the tanned carpet. Flinching from pains of the heart — emotional pains — nothing physical. He is a zombie walking towards the balcony door, his head wavering like a baby's as he glances around the room, finally ending his distorted focus on the low, cathedral ceiling.

Reaching the side door, he places both of his hands against the glass. He allows his head to fall forward, lightly banging against the transparent obstacle standing between him and the freefall of his life. Several times, his head and the glass meet — each one harder than the one before.

He unlocks the black, metal latch. With extreme effort, caused by the bare nothingness he feels in the pit of his stomach, he slides the glass door halfway open. Not needing any more space, he squeezes through the opening, immediately feeling the night's winds, playing along the strings of a delicate violin.

It's the world laughing at me. It doesn't stop to feel sorrow, or pity, or remorse… it simply moves right along. Leaving me alone, leaving me to trail behind in an entangled web of malevolent thoughts.

"I loved her. I loved her more than I've ever loved myself."

His arms limp at his side, he staggers to the edge of the balcony. He leans against the hand-carved railing, gripping the bars and peering over the edge. Flashy lights and illuminated skyscrapers dance around him in every direction. Below, an unforgivable fifteen stories down, the streets are full of zooming objects, their lights shining their ways.

He places his hands on the top of the rail, now beginning to elevate his body off the balcony. His feet are not touching anymore. Teetering along the safety banister, he pulls his body upward. Balancing and gathering a safe hold, he stands on the balance beam as though it was life's greatest challenge come forth.

Raising his arms above his head, he clinches his fists. He taps his forehead with

his closed hands — the devil's horns. With his
teeth grinding together, he shouts.

"WHY HER!"

And then Lucas limply plummets over the
edge—

My ex-friend killed himself, taking the easy way out from the pain that one's life can bring. Every being dealt with the horror, suffered the hardships, and had someone close to them die, but only the strong... only the ones who could block these horrifying images from surfacing on their own mind's X-ray screen could carry that happy demeanor day after day.

Henry Lucas didn't like the demons that stirred inside him—the demons that I've known since I was a young boy.

So, amidst a busy downtown New York, from his newly acquired loft, Hank ended it all. The great jump, with all the gory details, made the *Times*.

At least he had *that* added to his solid writing resume. One that wouldn't be receiving any calls any time soon.

T R A L O N
M O B C

chapter eleven

Morton Blacke looks up from the antique typewriter, watching as a redbird darts from one limb to the next outside in a rare-for-these-parts fig tree.

He stares out the window. His brain searches for the right words—the perfect finish to his epic manuscript. He couldn't complete something that had taken so much out of him—something that had been so highly anticipated—with a mere pule.

T.S. Eliot said, 'This is the way the world ends... This is the way the world ends... This is the way the world ends... Not with a bang. But with a whimper.'

Maybe so...

But not on this day. The page number—1,611—beckons from the top of the "special" order cream paper—no smear, no smudge—sticking above the typewriter's cylinder arm.

Morton raps his knuckles against the wooden desk. He has the last line of his masterpiece playing on a loop cycle inside his mind. He only needs the immediate words preceding the finale, a climax before the climax. And once those come, they will add the necessary enhancement and beam over a thousand pages of perfection.

And then...

And only then...

Morton Blacke will be able to type those magical "two words" that every great author dreams about.

You devilish son of a bitch you...

His fingers return to the keys. *They* may be cramping and sore, but the ivory ink-strikers never tire. One sentence and then another. And then another mesmerizing line filled with sharp wit combined with a puzzling oxymoron, only to be capped off with crisp and delightful bits of chicanery.

He pauses.

He's so eager, so ready, to type that closing sentence that is repeating... repeating... repeating... across the interior part of his forehead like a New York Stock Exchange ticker.

But he's not quite there, yet. He needs a final push. He needs a modicum more. His thoughts, however, are diverted by a passing image of Leslie.

He can smell her subtle, but captivating perfume. A fragrance, once combined with her beauty, that could force a man to throw away everything for her. He can taste her cherry lips. A tantalizing weapon against his own—soft and never boring. He can see her gorgeous, turquoise eyes looking deep inside of him with nothing to offer except pure love and admiration.

They had been together for over three months. The past couple had flown by along the wings of happiness, fast and wishing for more. Leslie had only left the 'Mansion on the Hill' a few hours earlier in the morning, heading to work. Staying over had become a frequent occurrence. In fact, neither Morton nor Leslie could even remember the last time they faced their sadness alone.

Most of her clothing, plus shoes, plus cosmetics, and even her blue and white curved toothbrush had found a new home in Morty's castle.

Sometimes, a minor break or deviation can assist a struggling writer by preventing them from forcing words or actions that don't quite fit.

It doesn't do you any good to try and fit the rectangular wood block through the crescent hole.

Morton's mind returns to last night—

He remembers laying in his massive bed, beneath the grand canopy, wearing a pair of black silk, robed pajamas with the letter 'B' embroidered in blood red above a left-hand pocket. He poses, relaxing on his side and leaving the mirror above to reflect an image he can't see. From around the bath area's opening, Leslie appears. Morton stares like a child eyeing the world's largest chocolate candy bar.

Leslie's honey-tanned legs glow, freshly shaved and well-oiled. They protrude from a lacy, bright blue pair of tiny panties, covering just enough to arouse one's curiosity—or arouse something. She models a matching bra, which reveals the top-halves of her full breasts, surprisingly maintaining that early twenties perkiness. Her face is as always to Morton Blacke—absolutely stunning. And her brown hair is tied in the back, allowing her bare shoulders and neck to show.

Leslie raises both of her arms, leaning against the doorway's right side. Her stomach, soft, but flat, displays signs of muscular toning. She removes the tie, tossing her head as her hair tumbles down her back and bounces over her shoulders like an erotic dancer weaving their spell of sex. She moves towards the bed like a ferocious tiger—a beast that walks on two legs.

She softly drops on the bed's edge, now crawling closer to Morton's side. Within range, he places his hands on her face, touching her with true warmth and then caressing her rosy cheeks.

They begin to kiss passionately and—

You foolish author! Why didn't you think of that sooner?

You must be getting old... getting rusty. Maybe you're just hitting that downward spiral that oh Henry Lucas talked about. Or maybe... hell, he's dead. I'm not.

Mr. Blacke types two quick sentences, several of the keys striking twice before getting a chance to even return to their starting position.

And right before he rises from his 'Medieval Throne,' pushing it away from the desk, to phone his agent, David Gregory, he types the words... *The End.*

b l a c k e

Many nights had been spent, since the completion of *All Roads Lead to Damascus*, brainstorming what to do next.

Morton didn't want to publish the novel. Something he recently began referring to as his "final triumph." He told Leslie that he would sign the manuscript over to her, and then, if something befell her before him, then it would belong to his agent. The reason: he wanted it to be published only after his own death.

That was his solution to the curse. That was his *only* solution. The post-release disease that struck those nearest to his heart; the part of his life that he had only shared with

Leslie Vitter.

But Leslie would have nothing of it. She, too, spent sleepless nights, restless and turning besides Morty, trying her best to think of an alternative fix. Time was running short on Morton's contract with Susperia Books. And he, above everything evil and wrong and morbid that had happened during his life, didn't want to break an agreement—an oath he made as strong as stone.

Unless, he chose not to release the novel... period. Until his death. But again, Leslie would have no part of this. She wanted to be in his life—forever. But she didn't want to be the reason he didn't unveil an unforgettable piece of literature that was guaranteed of being named his finest work yet. Leslie couldn't be held responsible for the "whimper." She would never let herself move forward if she metamorphosed from Morton's muse to his *writer's block*.

A mid-summer shower splashes against the 'Mansion on the Hill's' slate roof. Leslie lies on her back, Morton lightly snoring next to her. Her down pillows, of the higher thread count, how many she didn't remember, are soft beneath her head, but not comfortable enough to bring any sleep.

She loves this man. The words have yet to be spoken aloud, but she believes he feels the same. Leslie allows her left hand to rest on the side of his leg. She pats him, thinking, 'what are we going to do, Morty? What are we going to do?'

b l a c k e

The morning light couldn't have come any sooner.

At the crack of dawn, the first orange ray, tinted to the shade of Leslie's favorite juice, shines across the palatial landscape outside. The castle's guests, also beyond the outer walls, have come to life as well, chirping and calling the glorious unknown language of a new day—one Leslie hopes will help coax Morton away from the delicate stance he has previously taken.

She starts the morning off with a bang. "You're going to publish *All Roads*, hun. You know this, don't you?"

"Huh," Morton says, rubbing his crusty eyes. He sits up in the bed. He opens his right eye first, looking at Leslie with a comical grin. "What are you saying?"

"I said." Leslie puts her arms around him. "You're publishing *that* book. And not after you die, either. That's ridiculous."

She intends on being stern. She wants Morton to know the true value of her position. She needs him to understand the situation from her own perspective. He appears to be rattling the words around in his head. He scratches the side of his nose and then lightly fingernails his upper chest through a slot in his robe.

"Alright. If you say so."

Leslie starts to speak, but Morton presses two fingers against her morning-chapped lips. She waits for his direction.

"But," he begins, fingers remaining on her face, but now moving along her chin and neck. "We won't speak of it anymore today. We shall enjoy each other's company as before. Before this new problem surfaced. Before I spoke of... well... you know. Let's just make love this morning and then hit up Devil's Lake, whaddya' say?"

"Sounds wonderful."

b l a c k e

The water had gained some new color, a darker layer of green along the surface, and this wasn't a positive quality. Don't misunderstand. It wasn't filthy or unclean. It just wasn't the shimmering body of water that sparkled from the sun's rays like diamonds and was as translucent as freshly-

Windexed glass.

The rented yacht, white with black stripes, zooms across Devil's Lake at high speeds. Its man-made waves disturb a group of fishermen, casting erroneously from their two-seaters and smaller rafts. They can barely make out the name, *S.S. Miss Margaret*, painted along the large boat's starboard.

"I didn't know you knew how to run one of these things?" Leslie asks, talking loudly so the motor wouldn't drown out her question.

"And for the second time today, well... I do." Morton smiles as he remembers Leslie asking him that same question at the pier. He pulls a different lever than the one on his guest bedroom's wall, slowing the engine. "Here, take the wheel for a second."

"What? Where?"

"Straight for those rocks on the far bank."

"That sounds just great!" Leslie's sarcasm fills the moist air. A sour scent of fish and stagnant moss tickles her nose. Morton turns from the steering mechanisms and begins to descend the ladder leading to the deck.

"Yeah, I know," he says, carefully gripping the slick rungs. "But your supposed to stop the boat before getting to *those* rocks."

"Well shit... how do I do that?"

"Don't worry." Morton drops to the boat's main level, heading in the direction of the hatch door that takes him below. And fading out like a radio's volume being decreased, Morton adds, "I'll be back before you need me."

He momentarily disappears inside the belly of the boat. When he returns, his head, wind-blown hair and all, pops out of the hatch like a gopher's. He carries with him a bottle of *Dom Pérignon, Rosé Vintage 1996*, and two clear champagne flutes. He ascends the metal ladder, smiling as Leslie's head turns at a forty-five degree angle to see him arriving.

"Just in the nick of time," she says. Morton stands erect, peering down their path—the reflecting lake casts flickers of light like millions of slivers of broken glass bobbing amongst the tumbling rolls of water.

"Not even close," he says, handing over the bottle and glasses to Leslie. "Might want to wait on that, though. The proud Lago police think very highly of themselves. And they might enjoy writing up a famous writer for operating a yacht under the influence. See—" Morton points to the starboard side of the watercraft. "—there's one patrolling right there."

Leslie follows his direction with her eyes. She shakes her head, seeing a motorboat speeding towards them. She puts her left arm around the back of Morton's neck. "That boat there," she begins. "That's the head vet down at the clinic. Possibly with his wife and kids. Hardly the intimidating lake patrol."

"Whatever..." Morton's face reddens, but he is amused by the fatuous events. Leslie doesn't rub it in.

He steers the extravagant yacht along the western coastline, careful not to enter an area that's too shallow. He parks it in a shaded cove, the tall Evergreens and Douglas Firs protecting them from the sun's harsh light. The temperature seems to drop by ten degrees in a matter of minutes. The engine idles before he completely shuts down the boat. Morton then drops the anchor, securing the boat's location.

"Vould yew leke to jhoin mee on de dique, midam?" Morton asks, doing his best French accent.

"Évidemment," Leslie responds. No accent... the real thing.

"In that case... suivez-moi la belle dame." Morton touches her hand before carefully going down the slippery ladder. Once he feels his feet touch the wooden planks lining the boat's deck, he says. "I didn't know you knew French?"

"And I didn't know you knew French." Leslie holds up the champagne and glasses. "Why did you bring these up here?"

"Who knows?" Morton responds, shrugging. He then takes the alcohol, along with their special holders, from Leslie. He sets them down on the deck, reaching up to help his beautiful girlfriend down from the tricky yacht's cockpit. Once her footing is secure, he returns to the vintage necessities.

Together, embracing, they move to the front of the boat, where two bamboo loungers, with an umbrellaed center table awaits. Morton rests the tall champagne glasses in the middle of the table and pops the cork, drinking straight from the bottle like an experienced sailor. Leslie laughs, taking the glasses and holding them in front of his childish eyes.

Morton fills them all the way to the top, the bubbly liquid cascading over the glasses' edges like the hidden waterfall south of his home. They share more than drinks. They share laughter. They share an unexplainable ease and comfort that only comes from one being around the other. And Morton shares a childhood memory.

b l a c k e

"It was nineteen-seventy nine. Only one year since my dog, Smokey, had been hit by a passing car. Something that started so small... so... much like an accident that just happened to people, to animals. There shouldn't have been more behind it, but like I told you, my dear Leslie, there was. I knew it within my heart. I just knew it.

"And these feelings would carry on into different situations. That is... until I learned its true power within my writing. I learned it's true source.

"But that's a different story. One I've shared enough on... one better left in the past for now. The relevance of what I'm about to tell you seemed intertwined back then, but I now know it was only a case of bad luck. That, or a result of the foolish games we kids typically played. I can feel it now.

"On this day, I was thirteen years old and hanging out at Otter Creek with Jake... umm... Jake Cambers. Better known to us as Jake Snake. He was the starting pitcher on the baseball team. He was the first boy I knew to start kissing girls. We other kids didn't care at that time, but Jake certainly did.

"I had just gotten a brand new *Red Rider* BB gun for my birthday. Jake had already had one. And we wanted to both take them out and do us some shooting in the woods. Whatever moved, we opened fire. Birds. Rabbits. Squirrels. Even some of the catfish and smaller minnows were fair game. It didn't really matter, we wanted to fire our weapons.

And when that got boring, we decided to shoot at one another.

"I know, I know. It wasn't the brightest idea we'd ever had. Hell... it ended up costing Jake a lot more than just an irritating red dot on his skin. We each stood on our own side of the creek, firing back and forth and taking cover in some bushes or lying behind large logs. Neither one of us were wearing a shirt. Shit, we never did in those days. What was the good of wearing something you were only going to take off right before you dove into the cool water?

"Jake hit me in the left side, a BB ricocheting off my skin and leaving a stinging mark. It didn't feel good, but it hurt a hell of a lot less than a hardball. And within the next few shots, one of my BB's sailed high. They never flew straight anyways. And we weren't aiming for each other's heads. It just happened.

"The BB struck Jake Snake in his right eye. Perfect hit. Right square in the pupil before he could blink. The gunshot blinded him instantly. The poor kid, my dear friend, never saw out of that eye again. It ruined his pitching career, not to mention the fact he couldn't swing a lick at the plate, either. Man, I felt terrible.

"At first, I thought it was because I had gotten the *Red Rider* for my birthday. But I didn't feel *that* on my insides. It didn't feel the same as Smokey's death. And plus, I never wished for or dreamed about the gun. It was only a gift. No comparison to the Dwight Evans baseball card. That pretty much sums it up. And anyways, I thought I'd share it with you."

Leslie sips from her flute, emptying her second full glass. She doesn't say anything. She doesn't need to. Her eyes meet his, connecting upon an invisible channel. She only rises from her lounger and joins Morton in his. She snuggles up against his body, kissing his cheek and then lips.

"About the book—" Morton begins to speak, but Leslie quickly hushes him by leaning in for another kiss. She moves back a little, still feeling his breath on her skin.

"Not tonight, Morty. You made me promise. Not tonight."

The topic ends there.

The couple watches as the sun sets and the moon appears twice—twice as beautiful—once in the sky and another time on the water's surface. They make it just past midnight before starting up the yacht again and heading for the rental shop.

And yes... Leslie drives the entire way in. Morton beside her, guiding her, every wave of the way.

T R A L O N

M O B C K

chapter twelve

Sometimes I hated eating.

The food had become bland. My taste buds pretended to not exist. The unique tastes and smells faded behind a hazy cloud that suffocated all the wonderful flavors of the world. But I downed the sandwich regardless, layered with pastrami, provolone, lettuce, tomato, and a dab of chipotle-mayo. I chased it with a full glass of *Mount Veeder, Napa Valley*.

The temperature inside my dungeon mimicked winter's last call. Even though spring had arrived, an icy, still air hovered in the early mornings and late evenings. The chill touched my bare skin, arms and feet, causing me to shiver as I left the dining room's overbearing birch table behind.

I walked through the 'Great Passageway', heading out the front double doors. The oak creaked as good wood should, heavy, but swinging open as smooth as a carpenter's hammer flying through the air in search of another ringshanked nail.

A few night owls for birds whistled and sung, saluting my exit from the house. I walked down the white-rock steps, wary of the metal spires sharply poking above the support railing. Reaching the bottom, I made several aimless laps around the wishing well, that in my mind, could have been used to draw water for someone as mythically god-sized as King Arthur himself. Or perhaps, even Sir Lancelot. Or even better, maybe a magician like myself. Not one who *wrote* with magic, but spoke it and actually performed magical deeds—Merlin.

This thought bounced around in my brain like a beach ball, transcending me into another thought. I was reminded of one of my favorite characters, John Merlyn, in Mario Puzo's *Fool's Die*. I remember him being asked if his parents thought he would grow up to be a magician. 'No,' Merlyn had said, 'Merlyn's my last name. I changed it. I didn't want to be King Arthur, and I didn't want to be Lancelot."

Neither did I, my friend. Neither did I...

My bare feet grow sore from the paved driveway. I hadn't written on *All Roads Lead to Damascus* in a few weeks now, and feeling more than just delusional, my mind wandered.

Dreamlike—

It thought of my late wife, Sierra. It pictured her red Ferrari, motionless in the garage, covered in mounds of dust. It saw me stirring up the dust and causing a great, smoky commotion that followed with a coughing spell I didn't think I would ever recover from.

I heard my boy, Billy, calling 'Dad' from somewhere beyond the back of my mansion. He was likely playing near the crystal pond, chasing a flock of geese, and then I saw him diving in the refreshing drink.

Don't Billy! A voice in my mind shouted. *Stay away from the water!*

But it's too late. Someone else has already got him. *What are you doing, Professor Parkey? Don't swing Billy so high, you're going to hurt your back.*

My mentor ignored me. He and the boy played in the damp grass; his expensive brown khakis now featuring rich jade marks around the knees. He asked me why I named my boy 'William Blake?' And I kept telling him over and over again that I didn't. He told me to keep on writing... keep on with the rest of the world before it passed me by.

I didn't really care. Let them go. They don't know the way that I will travel. Their path was lost. Their leaders were corrupt, dishonest, and passionate about everything wrong in the world.

My way was the only way. I turned around, not wanting any more free advice for the day. I saw Jeffrey Jane walking up the driveway. He carried with him a dark backpack. He didn't wait for me to open the front 'B' gates. He moved through them like a ghost. He *spirit-walked* like the visitors in my mansion sometimes do, traveling between the walls from one room to the next. Without them, I would have nothing.

I try to tell Jeffrey that he's going the wrong way. He needed to come with me. Or better yet, he needed to just turn around and leave this god-forsaken place.

A loud bark stirred me from following my friend with my tired eyes. The bark comes again, splitting my skull in two, a deep crack beginning beneath my skin like a windy ravine cutting through the highest crests of the badlands.

I run back for the mansion. I run up the steps. I run through the oak doors. I disappear inside, not knowing if I closed the entrance or the spirits who walk with me made sure no one else entered.

The world was laughing. A fool of a famous writer who couldn't taste his food anymore. A silly author who couldn't even go into town, because the faces he might see could easily become bloodied and their bodies stiff once *All Roads Lead to Damascus* was finished. Was this what it had come to?

Was this the final time?

So many consequences...

So many decisions for someone who only wanted to write. I didn't believe I needed love. I didn't believe I needed friends. I didn't believe in anything anymore.

Except... of course.

Words on pages.

They were the only thing that mattered to me. They were the battery that charged my electric body. They were the fruit that filled my crepe. They were the Nightwatcher, winding the source connected to my heart, keeping me alive only to serve the purpose.

I staggered towards my office.

b l a c k e

The words moved across the page like a bulleting train heading East, row by row... line after line... one sentence and then another. I was working on my new masterpiece, maybe the last one, *All Roads Lead to Damascus*; already projected a bestseller by the likes of such prestigious newspapers as the *New York Times*, the *Washington Post*, and *USA Today*, to simply name a few.

The man turns... and there, standing behind him all smiles, the girl with the autumn-fire hair. Why would she be smiling? Why? After all that has happened to her in this demented world — this wretched town called Damascus.

No one really knows. This heart of man. The evil within, eating and stripping one's soul of their past premonitions without any cause, leaving a blackened void of ill-willed deceit. The fear rises in the pit of his stomach as the girl — all smiles — continues to arouse his persistent curiosity. He opens his mouth to speak. Nothing.

She turns away from him, and then calmly says these words, beneath her breath. "You never should have—"

The loud, thunderous clang of bronze meeting ancient oak disrupted my thoughts. I stopped typing on my antique typewriter, a family heirloom passed through generations. It was my favorite keepsake. The crisp keys whiter than any I had ever seen before, capped with a perfectly thick layer of enhanced ivory. It was my favorite device for putting words to pages. Forgotten was the computer. I cocked my head in the direction of the mansion's vast foyer, something I liked to call the 'Great Passageway' leading to the many doors of my realm.

What time is it? I thought, lifting my fingers from the keys for the first time in hours. *I know I left the gates open for some reason... just can't remember why?* I stretched my hands wide as if I were ready to crush someone's skull. I then leaned back in my 'Medieval Throne,' another pet name for something a little less dramatic. Although, my "writing" chair was rather overwhelming, with its back-lined, crushed red velvet and its jewel-encrusted wooden arms and legs. Throwing my arms into the air like a prophet beckoning to the gods, I rocked forward out of the "throne" and stood.

For the second time, the banging on the front door startled me. *I'm coming... I'm coming.* Leaving my octagon-shaped office, on the west wing of the mansion, I headed through a door to the northern part of the house before turning to my right down a long, narrow hallway, lined with glass-cased shelves, dust free, carrying shadowbox-themed memoirs and my lifetime of writing accolades. These memoirs, unlike the east wing, carried only my past, and not my family's. This hallway, although notoriously long day or night, seemingly grew and haunted as the hour passes and the light from the west window shone no more.

But daylight had just begun, as scattered strands of the sun's beams portrayed a shadow on the wooden-planked floor before the traveling writer that was me. It wasn't too long ago when this constricted hallway echoed with a child's laughter. But that was just a faded memory of what was… and what would never be again.

The knocking occurred a third time; I shook my head as I came to another door at the end of the hall. *A little patience my persistent friend.* This door opened into the 'Great Passageway,' and the I turned to my right again and proceeded to the front of the luxurious mansion. I arrived at the main entrance, which towered above any six-foot person, with heavy oak double-doors and a half-circle finish at the peak; one might have thought there would be a portcullis and a moat waiting outside.

I raised the rustic iron latch, drawing free the lock, and then tugged on the circular brass handle (appearing like a bull's nostril ring) fastened to the door to my right, and the visitor's left. The door slowly cracked open, revealing new light in the mansion's foyer. Before me stood a nervous-looking fellow with a pen in one hand and a clipboard full of papers in the other. A reflecting piece of a silver recorder exposed itself at the top of his tan, sport's jacket's chest pocket. Sweat beaded on his balding head, running down his forehead and into his beady eyes behind his perfectly-round rimmed glasses.

"Mr. Blacke?"

T R A L O N
M O B C K E

chapter thirteen

A dense fog, full of an autumn mist, envelops the mansion's surrounding hills.

Blurred lights shine through the infamous 'B' gates, their brilliant bulbs dulled by the eerie weather. The driver sees no intercom, so he waits. And after five minutes or so of no activity—no open gates—the driver taps on his horn.

Leslie, who is preparing breakfast in the "safe" kitchen, kitchen "número uno," peers over the tops of the swinging doors to the dining room.

"Who could that be?" she asks.

Morton sets down the *Lago Diablo News* on the enormous dining table, takes a quick sip of his black coffee, and then answers, "I haven't the slightest clue."

He walks closer to her, leaving his warm drink and daily read behind.

"Maybe we should see?" Leslie asks, but before her favorite companion can answer, her eyes bulge with excitement. Something has triggered the possible answer to her question. "I know! It's probably the movers!"

Morton tweaks his head. "What is today?"

"The ninth," Leslie answers.

"What month?" Morton asks, this time obviously—hopefully—joking.

"October, silly."

Morton stands. He motions for Leslie to remain in the kitchen, saying, "I'll take care of it. Please keep on cooking those scrumptious omelets with five layers of different meats and oh my."

Leslie giggles at his thorough instructions and returns to the stainless steel stove. Morton heads for the garage, needing a remote for the gates. Once he is finally outside, close enough to open them via a click of the button, he whistles—two fingers in his mouth—and motions for the moving truck to enter. He isn't sure whether they can even see him, not with the lingering morning fog still layered near earth's floor.

The movers, with Morton's guidance, park in front of the white-rock steps. The side of their van reads, *"We can move a Wicker-ton."* This amusing play on words, using the neighboring town, causes Morton to chuckle every time.

The driver steps out.

"How's it hangin', Mr. Blacke?" the man asks, a wad of

dip tucked into his bottom lip. He isn't the most formal of Morton's semi-friends.

"Mostly to the right," Morton responds, encouraging the driver.

"Long as dem' ain't danglin' to you'z left," the man says, sticking out his gloved hand. "We might thinks you be a lil' queer, huh Tommy."

The driver's helper, a boy barely eighteen, if that, wearing a Beantown baseball cap, has stepped out of the passenger side of the van and nods. Morton shakes the man's hand.

"We wouldn't want that now," he says, finishing the comedy segment. "How's it coming, Sal?"

Salvatore Diego, a man in his early fifties, one who, a few years back, had helped Morton install his magnificent birch table before the walls went up, was still able to work harder and faster than those twenty years younger. He pats his friend on the back and says, "Same shit, different day."

Sal motions for his helper to open the back of the van. He turns back to Morton and says, "Not much stuff in there. We only gots the thangs that were marked."

"Yeah... I know," Morton fills in the driver. "The rest of the furniture is for sale with the house. It's a packaged deal. Misty Lane will never be the same."

"If you says so."

The moving crew of two begin unloading Leslie Vitter's most valuable—most collectible—goods, carrying them into the mansion. The morning moves fast, Leslie now leading the charge as Morton finishes reading the paper.

After all the items are inside, the couple sit down at the dining table and enjoy their omelets and juice together. Morton's three-egg, monster dish, features bacon, ham, Italian sausage, pepperoni, turkey, colby jack cheese, swiss cheese, jalapeños, olives, onions, mushrooms, and tomatoes. Leslie's two-egg, all-whites, only has turkey, swiss cheese, and the veggies.

The rest of the day passes uneventful. Just two lovers enjoying one another's company.

b l a c k e

"I've got it!" Morton shouts from his sleep, snapping forward in his oversized bed. Leslie, startled from her nightly slumber, looks up at him. Morton stares deep into her eyes. He repeats himself for her.

"I've got it, my darling!"

b l a c k e

A few months have passed since Morton's exciting reverie.

Susperia Books had, with both his and Leslie's approval, moved forward with the release of *All Roads Lead to Damascus*. This is the way they wanted it. As Morton worked in the office and Leslie folded some of her clothes upstairs, the 'Mansion on the Hill' had been quiet, that is, before...

Leslie's red cell phone begins to ring with the theme from *Phantom of the Opera*.

"Hello," she answers, unsure of the caller with a New York area code.

"Hey Leslie, it's Dave."

The agent...

"Oh, hey. How are you doing?" she asks.

"I'm doing fine," David Gregory responds. "I tried calling the house, but of course, no one answered."

"Yeah, well... you know how it is. Morton and his lever."

"Yes, trust me. I know." A slight pause. And then David asks, "Is Morton around? I've got some news for him."

"Sure... let me get him." Leslie leaves the master bedroom, heads through the landing, down the spiral skeleton stairs, across the foyer to the door leading to the west wing hallway, down the long corridor, and finally arrives at the octagon office. She knocks on the door.

"Come in," A muffled voice sounds from within the room. Leslie opens the door and enters. Morton Blacke sits at his desk, working on something new. It could be just simple notes. But who knows? It could be something more.

"David Gregory is on the phone."

"Oh, sure." Leslie hands him the cell. She looks out his office windows, admiring the winter view. Flurries upon flurries of different shapes and sizes of white snowflakes pass outside the glass dividers on their way to the join the crunchy layers of snow already resting on the ground. Icicles dangle from naked trees, some longer than a foot in length. A newly acquired birdbath, made of a rich-stained pewter, something Leslie had added to the mansion's lawn, is frozen over.

Morton's voice disrupts her dreamlike journey—an out-of-body experience—through winter wonderland.

"Hey there, Dave. What's the word?"

"Got some good news, Morton. Or should I call you... *Tralon*. You jumped into the top ten on the bestseller's list. I sent an overnight copy of the *Times* article, you should have it by now. Anyways, how 'bout that?"

"That's just wonderful," Morton says, looking down at a copy of his newest release, lying on the desk to the right of his antique typewriter. *All Roads Lead to Damascus*, by Tralon Mobcke. "Who would have ever thought an unknown author, a first-timer, would have gotten that far up?"

"Not me," Gregory answers. "I know I was very skeptical, well... downright negative to start. But things have turned out pretty good. You are a fantastic writer, Mister Blacke."

It is the first time David Gregory ever used *mister* before his name. Morton smiles. "Don't you mean Mister Mobcke?"

"I don't give a shit who the authors name is. It's a bestseller."

"It sure is..." Morton trails off. He stares out the window, looking at the same winter scene Leslie is, neither of them aware of the other's parallel eyes.

"Gotta' run, Morton. I'll give you another update soon."

"Alright, Dave. Thanks for the call."

"No problem. You all have a wonderful day."

"You, too. Talk to you later."

"Okay. Bye Morton."

"Bye Dave."

Morton hangs up the phone. Leslie stands beside him, leaning against the desk. She taps her foot impatiently, waiting for her "Mobcke" to speak.

"Guess what?" Morton asks.

"What?"

"Stay right here. Don't move." Morton hops out of his throne. He hurries to the exit door, sprinting down the west wing's hallway. Leslie remains behind, more out of bewilderment at what is transforming, than actually following orders. Morton darts through the mansion's oak doors. He runs by the medieval wishing well, heading for the front gates. He drops to one knee, reaching his right arm through the bars as far as it could possibly stretch, barely able to grasp yesterday's addition of the *New York Times*.

He runs back to the house, carrying the newspaper under his right arm. Once back inside, he struggles to catch his breath—rapid gasps follow a deep oxygen intake. He keeps moving. Back to the office. Back to Leslie.

He unfolds the paper before her curious eyes.

"What is it?" she asks, excited and eager to see for herself.

"There," Morton says, pointing to the upper-left

column of a page in the *entertainment* section.

In the *New York Times*, just below six books and six names, including King, Grisham, and Brown, the following appears:

#7 - *All Roads Lead to Damascus*, by Tralon Mobcke

b l a c k e

Morton stares at the computer screen, an early Christmas present from Leslie.

The cursor flashes at him, on... off... on... off. The frustration from trying to solve something new—something the world has fully accepted—is written all over his face. He uses the tip of his index finger to move the guiding arrow around the page. Nothing makes sense to him.

Music, coming from a CD that Leslie had earlier placed in the hard drive, plays from the laptop's speakers.

Morton listens to Simon & Garfunkel's *Greatest Hits*, thinking...

I might not know how to work this thing, but at least I've got The Boxer.

Leslie enters the office.

"You know," Morton begins. "I've been deemed a genius before, but this is beyond my grasp."

"Come on, hun, you'll get it. You've just got to be patient. Give it some time."

"Plus," Morton's trivial complaining continues, "My typewriter is really, really lonely. We've been through a lot together. I consider him a very dear friend."

"I just thought," Leslie pauses. She acts as though a heavy sneeze is coming, holding her nose and mouth, but then it passes—no cause for alarm. "I thought that with a new start and all, for Tralon Mobcke, and a new era of writing, you might want some change. A fresh beginning with an upgrade."

Morton smiles at her. Leslie's thoughtful and heartfelt intentions were more than he could have ever hoped for in his life. He closes the computer screen and the music disappears. "I know, dear. Your gift is wonderful, and I know you mean well. I'll give it another shot tomorrow."

Morton hugs Leslie. She wraps her arms around him and squeezes tightly, feeling his grip strengthen as well. The hold isn't unbearable, just comfortably snug. Morton releases and takes one step backward. A piercing look beams from his licorice eyes and slanted brows—a row of hard wrinkles line his forehead. He says, "I need to go do something."

"Yeah? Need help?" Leslie, with combined curiosity and sincerity, asks. She is unsure of the scared expression.

"Not for this one, my sweet, irreplaceable Leslie. *This...* I must do alone. I won't be long. I promise," he pauses. "And when I return, everything will be right again."

"Where are you going?" Leslie questions, a look of slight concern now arises on her face.

"Not far."

Morton begins to leave the office. Leslie's voice stops him. "Morty?"

He turns around, standing in the doorway, and says, "Please don't worry. I'll explain everything in due time."

Leslie watches as he disappears down the west wing hall. She doesn't follow him. Instead, she reopens the computer, deciding to do some trial and error herself, already having plenty of experience from working with the clinic's computers.

Mr. Blacke heads towards the east wing. He stops in its mirror hall—a near-perfect reflection to the west side of the mansion, only the content on the shelves differed. The pictures of his past wife have been removed. Some new framed photos of Leslie and him have taken their place. But smiling images and playful escapades of William Blacke remain. He peers at one picture in the upper left of the glassed shelves, it is of Billy as an infant, bundled up in a baby outfit that matched his dad's own robe in another photo immediately to its right. Mr. Blacke searches near the middle of the setup, seeing another picture of Billy, a happy child, laughing as he appeared to be tearing the pages out of one of his dad's own novels. *Every Dog Has Its Night.* Adjacent to that image, Mr. Blacke sees a newspaper clipping with a photo of him and his son high-fiving at Times Square. Mr. Blacke scans one last scene: Billy playing with blocks on the floor in his playroom, something the boy liked to refer to as *his office.*

'Daddy's offiss is on dee udder side of dee house,' he had once said. 'Dis is my offiss.'

Mr. Blacke moves on. He takes a few steps towards the garage, before halting in front of a closed door on his right. He grabs the bronze knob and turns it to clockwise. He pushes inward. The door squeaks like a trapped mouse—it seems to scream with pain from not being used in a very, very long time.

Streams of light enter through gaps in the windows' closed blinds. The subtle breeze from the door's opening stirs the dust, their particles appearing in the lighted areas and then fading away. It doesn't mean they aren't there; they are just hiding in dark corners.

Three long toy boxes line the octagon walls under the windows. They serve as low benches, until one need be opened. The other walls are fronted with fancy bookshelves, some used for children's books, and others for holding displayed figurines and stuffed animals and other creatures. A large, padded rug designed with a custom map of the five towns, Lago Diablo in the center, rests on the hardwood floor.

Billy loved to race his cars down 163, thinking of the route, which should be a loop, as a giant racetrack.

"My fucking writing. My damned... brilliant... novels. My son's life."

Mr. Blacke lifts the lid of the toy box in the middle. Taped to the underbelly of the wooden cover is a small key. He pulls it from the tape and then bends down nearer the center of the playroom. He grabs the corner of the map rug and begins to roll the edge. Halfway folded, the floor reveals two black hinges and a small, flat latch. He pushes the rug aside and pulls the latch upward. The hardwood trapdoor opens, a two-foot deep hole appears, cut out of the earth and cemented. More dust rises, causing Mr. Blacke to sneeze twice. Once recovered, he looks into the secret spot. The only item inside the opening is a small bag, knotted closed with a neon green string.

"There you are," he speaks aloud, alone.

Mr. Blacke grabs the bag and closes the trapdoor. He returns the rug to its original location and then stands. On his way out of the room, he catches a glimpse of a familiar hero—a framed baseball card of Dwight Evans hanging on Billy's wall. Mr. Blacke tips his imaginary ballcap to the Red Sox outfielder and then exits the playroom, closing the squeaky door behind him. He heads towards the center of the mansion. He turns to his right, passing through the dining area and moving to the 'Evil Kitchen.' He exits the mansion through the back door on the east side, leaving the West, and all of its pleasantries and warmth behind. He confronts the demon on its turf. He bites his lip, tasting blood, and smiles. He isn't scared anymore. God only knows, he wants to go home.

He carries the money bag in his right hand, walking like a dead man towards the elegant pond. He crosses the snowy meadow, shivering for the first time. Mr. Blacke's unprotected face, arms, and bare feet add some color as the cold nips at his heels. He can feel the snow crunch beneath his exposed souls, numbing the toes first, and then moving deeper, nearer the arches.

He moves forward, his pace never slowing, and reflects on the life he has lived—

Mr. Blacke. Full of surprises. Full of mysteries. Full of peculiar habits and hidden agendas. All for everyone else's well being and safety. All for everyone else. But not those dearest. Not those closest to the invisible demons within me.

Selfish?

Greedy?

Misled?

I feel pain. I feel more than you know. The mansion is changing around me. I've been inside those walls, but they are changing. They will not be a part of my skin, a seed that grows beneath the outer layers, never again.

Wake demons.

Wake and watch...

The Mr. Blacke you bastards know all too well... not anymore. I've got a surprise for you.

Mr. Blacke arrives at the pond's edge. A paper thin layer of ice floats on the water's surface, cracked in several places—levitating shards of translucent glass. Shadows dance across the white as a gusty frost passes. The temperature continues to fall as the sun drops out of view, hiding for today but promising a return tomorrow.

Mr. Blacke stands, motionless.

Without a single word. Without a single thought. No witty saying or cinematic farewell. No warning. No nothing.

Mr. Blacke raises his right arm and throws the money bag—its deception and guilt—into the center of the pond. Pieces of ice break and look like tiny bergs being pushed in every direction by a tidal wave as the bag splashes in the water and sinks below. Once hidden from view, Morton smiles.

Swallowing his trepidation, he turns and heads for home. He crosses the first part of the meadow with his face down, shielding against the cold air. Halfway there, he looks up.

He sees Leslie staring out the 'kitchen number one'—the 'Good Kitchen'—window. Tender eyes, grouped with a caring look of confusion amid all the love in this relationship spells out everything.

That's where I need to be, Morton thinks. *That's where I belong.*

He enters the mansion through the back door on the west side. Leslie is there, waiting for him with an Indian blanket of multiple colors of the outdoors, and a warm cup of hot chocolate.

"Hurry inside, you are going to freeze to death," she says, wrapping the hand-sewn material around him. The couple moves to the dining room, sitting in silence. No words need be spoken. It isn't awkward or uneasy. It is perfectly comfortable and calm. Leslie thinks about asking him what he has been doing outside, but she knows he will tell her when the time is right.

They sit until night falls, substituting hot chocolate for coffee. With emptied mugs and warm bellies, another day draws nearer to its end. And then Morton breaks the mold. "Ready for bed?" he asks.

"Yes, hun," she says. Leslie feels that with a new light, Morty will reveal today's events, and they will be the end of the end—where so many steps in a person's life are only the beginning of the end. An empty promise. A half-hearted commitment to change. She knows Morton Blacke is different. She feels it more than anything she's ever felt before. They head to the bedroom and change into their sleeping attire.

Once resting in the softness of *their* massive bed, snuggling beneath the warm sheets and padded comforter, they can fully relax, allowing the world around them to keep busy and stress over trivial matters.

The room is dark. The winter night is quiet.

"I love you," Morton says, the words escaping his mouth are never truer.

"I love you, too," Leslie responds. She kisses Morty good night. A flash of light illuminates the room—a winter storm is brewing. With nature's glow...

He looks in the mirror, knowing her eyes are looking as well. He sees himself smiling because...

He's Mr. Blacke...

And you're not—

Those magical two words...

THE END

<u>Other Books by Reagan Rothe</u>

Misanthropy: Book I: The Tower

Misanthropy: Book II: The Cellar Door

Misanthropy: Book III: The Window (Coming soon...)

Dreams and Baseball, Top of the Inning

Dreams and Baseball, Bottom of the Inning (Coming Spring 2011)

Give Wings to My Triumph

Reagan Rothe not only writes books, but he publishes them as well. *Blacke* is his fourth full-length novel, and it strongly indicates the range of his writing capabilities and the deviating styles he has been able to portray.

He currently resides with his beautiful and amazing wife, Minna, in Castroville, TX. He is a frequent public speaker on the publishing world and what it takes to be a thick-skinned author—focusing on positivity.

Rothe spends his non-writing time either outdoors on the trails, mountain biking, or watching sports—the Texas Longhorns, Dallas Cowboys, and Yankee baseball.

Please visit www.rothebooks.com for information on Rothe's ongoing book tour, scheduling news, and future releases.